Whip Han

Two Novellas of Female Supremacy

By
Miss Irene Clearmont

FDC

1st Edition

For author information contact:

Miss Irene Clearmont:
Contact Address: www.MissIreneClearmont.com
Email Comments: Irene@MissIreneClearmont.Com

“No matter what they say. It's all about money. So let's imagine, ladies, that you're a savings and loan officer. Watch… one, two, three. See! You've got it all, and we've got nothing.”

A Magician (1990)

Contents

“Whip Hand”

Whip Hand

A gentle sea breeze came in from the sea. It whispered up the beach where the tide was receding and then climbed to move the fronds of the palms that grew on a concealed loggia overlooking the azure Pacific Ocean.

A single leather sofa, set so as to display the spectacle of the rollers, held just one occupant, an almost naked woman who sat with a cocktail in her hand and looked down at the man who lay fettered at her feet. The small smile on her lips was not reflected in her eyes, it was just a small sign to her helpless companion that she was satisfied with his conduct and so would soon require some intimate service from him.

"I think you know why I allowed you here?" she said.

Though the question was purely rhetorical, he was not permitted to answer her unless explicit permission was given for him to speak.

That acquiescence was not liable to be forthcoming!

He did not move, but just kneeled by her shapely legs and waited for a direct command. From where he kneeled he could see the delicate perfect folds of her sex, the rounded breasts and porcelain smooth skin. There was no sign of his awareness of the aloof sexuality oozing from her every pore. That was the way that he had been trained by her – with the help of the physical restraint that caged him and allowed no indication of an erection to annoy her.

The surf broke on the rocks of Ocean Cove and Cynthia contemplated the sea, admiring the stark plainness of the panorama. Just a few whitecaps that scored lines of an endless surface of blue that stretched to the obscure line of the horizon. A line that defined sea and sky and set them apart.

With care she bent to place her glass on the ground and picked up the small dictation recorder that lay by her side and held it up for his inspection. His eyes followed the movement of her hand and then flickered to meet hers for a moment before lowering and fixing on the stilettos that were the only thing that she had chosen to wear.

"I understand that you have finished the small task that I set a week ago," she said as she held up the recorder. "It was the last time that you are to be permitted to speak freely, so I really hope that you made the most of it! I am not ungenerous and you will not be punished for the remarks that you voiced."

Her finger twitched and the man's recorded voice stammered from the recorder:

"I am Ray Lever," *the husband's voice began.* "This is the story of my abiding love for my wife Cynthia…"

Cynthia switched off the recorder for a moment and crossed her legs to present the sharp spike of her shoes to the lips of the man. He did not move and she nodded a small acknowledgement of her approval before she allowed her heel to slip from the shoe to leave it dangling on her toes.

"You may," she said to her husband.

It was not a suggestion, it was an imperative! He responded by kissing the spike of the shoe with a delicate almost loving brush of his lips. Now that the scene was set, she flicked the recorder on again and concentrated on the tone of his voice…

*****

I know perfectly well that everyone that I know considers Cynthia to be a trophy wife. A clever, intelligent, superior trophy, but a trophy nevertheless. I know that they think that she came from nothing, from the streets, that she caught me in her toils and then married into my money. She was never on the street, she never sold herself under the transit arches or hopped into a man's car for twenty dollars!

I know that they all think that there is a pre-nup, that I would not be so totally stupid as to fail to protect my money, my business and my future from a hungry whore. They are absolutely right there is a pre-nup…

I know what is what, I know what I want.

What I need to do is to set the record straight, I want the world to know that I opened a door in my psyche that I could not close again.

Do I regret it?

Well, you'll see, because I am allowing you, the listener, through that door as well, to see where the skeletons are buried. Most of all I know that the only person who will hear this is my wife… or at least I am fairly sure, because this is for her even if I call her by name because it is something that is a mark of respect that she deserves.

I am starting to ramble… how can I help it?

This is my testament to the woman that I am obsessed with!

The woman who I long to be allowed near, the woman who moves me to hope.

I want her to feel my feelings and love my loves, but she never will, because to her I am just a man to be used and abused. Thrown away when she is finished with me, a man who just wants to be near her.

Cynthia came through my front door and rearranged the house of my mind. Now, even for me, it is just like visiting a museum. Every case is filled, labelled and ready for inspection, but no-one cannot change my life now for a simple reason. She placed everything in its proper place.

If you are listening to this, then I am probably no longer here, well let's put it this way, I am no longer Ray Lever!

I know that certain of my relatives, perhaps my friends, business associates and many people who thought I was one thing, will now find out that I am another. They all understood why I married Cynthia, how could any man resist that beauty? How could any man other than hope that he would be invited into her bed? It was my hope too! I too had my obsessions, I thought that I could bottle them and allow them out on weekends, but it seems that they could not be contained.

I thought that I could conceal who I was.

There will be nothing left of all those riches that I earned from my silly software. Not a nickel... why? Because Cynthia will get it all, she is the only person who meant *everything* to me. Former wives, parents and friends... they all came and went, they all took what they thought that they deserved from me and left the rest. Cynthia was the only person who took me as I was and then siphoned it all off.

Every drop.

I know that she will have it all, because if that is what she wants she will surely find a way to get it. I love you Cynthia, I know you, I respect and serve and I promise that... well let's leave that for the ending.

What she did not like she changed.

That was her way, that was her vision and I was just the man who paid everything he had for what she was offering…

*****

I shall begin at the beginning!

The beginning is not my birth, it is not my childhood, it is certainly not my education, my brief sojourn in Yale. It is not the start of my business creating and selling a small application for computers that allows people to bypass paying for their calls. I have long since sold *most* of the rights to that work, but I still have a five per cent share that brings in more money a year that any sane man could spend in a lifetime. So I shall start with none of those irrelevant fragments of my life.

I did not become who I am in all those phases of my life. They were tiny quanta, but never totally significant. Nothing changed as it did when I met Cynthia, the owner of my life.

So, where does the story begin?

Here.

I was in a restaurant, whose name I do not recall, in New York. It was just off Times Square and if I remember aright all the waiters and waitresses burst into song every now and again while they served the weak coffee and tired pancakes. I was there with Florence, my ex-wife, and my brother.

I suspect that the two of them were trying to inveigle me into hooking up with her again, but I avoided striking the ball against the moving bat and evaded all attempts to make me repeat the mistake that I had made just three years ago. I was enjoying my freedom from partnership as well as the fact that business was going so well that I was starting to have to hide my income from Florence as well as everyone else who felt that they should reap from the fictitious relationship 'investments' that they had made in my life.

I drank my coffee. I ate the rather soggy pale pancakes with their 'simulated' maple syrup and paid only half an ear to Florence who had determined that I would love to reacquaint myself with her rather tired social circle.

"It's grand opera of the best sort," she said. "Three hours of Verdi followed by a marvelous opportunity to network with some of the richest people in New York."

How could she possibly know that I was already one of the richest men in New York already? With my app almost sold, the rights and patents all sealed up tight like a drum and my partners bought out for a measly three million dollars.

My greedy brother joined in.

Now it was clear that he was in cahoots with Florence.

"I was going to partner Florence, but how would that look?" he said.

What I wanted to say was, 'It would look like you were fucking the cunt, that's what it would look like,' but that would not have been politic at all so I simply said, "I really think that you should stick to that plan!"

He looked at me, obviously confused. Was I saying that he should go with my ex, or was I saying that he should keep trying to persuade me?

In the end he looked at her and she shook her head ever so slightly as if to say, 'Forget it, he's never going to go for it…'

So I sat there and let them play out their little drama.

My brother, the wastrel who thinks that as older brother he is a pillar of wisdom that I have to lean on and Florence who had probably heard a rumour that I had found another female partner at long last.

Not true.

I sipped my coffee.

At last my brother sighed and said, "You know, Ray, you'll *never* find a better partner than Florence."

"Oh," I replied, "I thought that you had found her now!"

That was pretty much the end of the little attempt to get me back with a woman who thinks that books are something to steady a table with a short leg and that Chinese food must be imported from the Far East. So, Bro' got all argumentative, Florence got all superior and I was left in that godforsaken bar listening to the waiters sing the latest song from some shit revival Broadway show.

It was then that I took the decision.

To go to that performance of Aida and show her that the last person that I needed on my arm was a greedy ex-wife. A brainless woman who would just bathe in the whispered rumours and revel in the notoriety of catching her ex in her toils again.

There was of course a problem, to wit: I had no partner!

So I decided to solve my problem in the innovative way that I was coming to solve all my problems. Money! I decided to pay for a companion, a woman of mystery, a gorgeous belle unknown to society. This companion that I would buy would just be so stunning that all heads would be turned, all eyes would be raised to our box and of course all imaginations would be running at overload.

All that I needed to do was to find her.

*****

Times Square is no longer the degenerate plaza that it used to be. That does not mean, however that past grime has entirely vanished. There are still a few girls to be found wandering the streets, spending their time trying to decide if you are a plain clothes cop and if you are worth propositioning.

I saw a couple of them, tired meat. At any rate I thought that perhaps they were whores, perhaps not. It does not really matter, because it was the idea that made me laugh out loud rather than that I saw a perfect woman for my scheme.

So I stayed in a hotel.

I had a small apartment in New York, just an open plan room with a bed and an Internet connection, but a hotel was so much more fitting. I checked in and used the browser on my phone to find an escort. At the time it seemed a better way than to just pick up someone in the street. I flicked through all the escorts that they had on parade and tried to imagine which would be suitable.

In the end I plumped for Cynthia. She spoke three languages and was stunningly attractive in almost every department. Cynthia was just five foot and a single inch tall and was dressed in a shiny tight material that was more revealing than all the bikinis and lace that the others on that escort site were wearing.
Nakedly covered, concealing exposure!

It was not as if I was looking for a sexual adventure anyway, I just wanted a woman who would make Florence gasp with resentment as we entered the Metropolitan.

Half an hour later I was in a bar by Central Park waiting at a table for the woman who charged a thousand dollars an hour, even if she was just drinking coffee. I whiled away the time calculating how long a million dollars would last and came to the conclusion that my last wife had cost me about the same per hour as the woman who was arriving soon. As long as I had just spent a couple of hours a day with Florence, that is.

My first sight of Cynthia was her walking past the window of the bar. She was short, but perfectly formed! Her hair was braided into a single long plait that hung down the back of her fur coat and her shoes were the highest stilettos that I had ever seen. When she turned to face me, she had one of those round faces, lush with full lips that is not immediately beautiful, but has a lustful and voluptuous draw to it that is pure sex. Those kissable lips; of course they were redder than poppy and her eyelashes were drawn into long strands that glistened with crystal dust.

She was perfect; at least I thought so at the time!

"So you just want the most expensive coffee in New York then?" she asked as she swept her coat with a hand and slid into the table opposite me.

"Well, let's say that it's the most expensive job interview then!"

The waitress arrived. My vision of feminine loveliness did not even look at her, she just said, "Espresso ristretto," and a twitch of a smile turned up one side of her lips.

"Are you living in the eighties then?" she said.

"Pardon?"

"Pretty Woman, made in nineteen eighty nine, man needs prostitute as escort and then marries her. They all live happily ever after as far as I can remember."

I started to laugh, it had never occurred to me that I was playing the script of some film.

"Nineteen ninety, I think," I said. "But, otherwise you are right. The difference is that I have no intention of starting out our little business association with a furious weekend of sex first!"

"Then we are on the same wavelength," she said as the coffee arrived. "I have never had intercourse with any of my clients and I have no intention of starting now! Anyway you are scarcely Richard Gere!"

The couple on the table behind her were all ears! I could see the woman lean back a little and incline her head to listen.

"That's fine," I replied. "No fucking then, how about something other than intercourse be on the cards? Would a blow job be possible?"

Cynthia started to laugh and picked up the tiny cup of coffee.

"I do all sorts of things and have been known to be generous, but I take it that you read the page on my blog?"

"Blog?"

"Yeah, my blog. I write all about my experiences, some of them are real, some are pure fantasy and others are start as the truth and end as exciting little white lies. That, of course, is where you find out that I am in the business of pain and anguish."

"You mean that you are a dominatrix?"

"Tsk, tsk," she said as she finished her coffee, "That's a very *plastic* word for what I am usually paid to do. I am a cause of anguish that men love and need. At least when I am not being paid to drink coffee and be overheard by the prurient, prejudging, moralistic cunts on the next table!"

The woman on the next table started and then slowly leaned forward to speak to the man who was with her. They left with a scraping of chairs and looks that were all contempt on her part and sheer lust on his.

"That's fine," I said.

"Good, then you can pay me the thousand for this little chat. You have forty minutes left and then I have to be somewhere. Incidentally, you have not paid for honesty, so don't bother asking me personal questions!"

"What are you doing next week, Monday in the evening?"

"I am free, well at least I should say that I am at liberty to meet with you. We could do business if you are ready to pay my fee."

I reached into my pocket and pulled my wallet from my pocket. A thousand dollars is only ten notes, they did not lie on the table for long at all.

"You have my attention," she said as she slid the money into a pocket of the fur coat. Every now and again I caught a glimpse of the dress that she wore under the coat.

Shiny!

Latex.

"The opera, Aida to be exact," I said.

"That's just less than three hours *and* the interval," she said. "Then we have to meet and go together and possibly there is a small function after the show?"

"Possibly…"

"That means that you will be paying me fifteen thousand for the night plus the prices for everything else. Tickets, limousine, food, drinks and clothes."

"You want me to pay for a dress?"

"Of course! How can a woman go to the opera in any old rag?

"OK, then I'll pay the dress as well. How much?"

“Give me twenty and the deal is sealed,” she said.

“Fine,” I answered as she glanced at her watch. “There is something else as well… No other appointments that evening!”

“I *never* see more than one client a day, an hour, ten hours, it makes no difference. One client a day maximum.”

“Then its set,” I said.

“Not quite… do you want me in fetish and fur,” she said as she slowly opened her coat to reveal the skin hugging latex body suit that lay underneath. “Or something more conventional?”

“Whatever you look best in,” was my reply, but I hoped for the latex and fur.

Florence would go wild with envy and my stupid brother with lust.

“Latex it is then,” she laughed. “Just give me your number and I’ll call to tell you how to pay. It’s got to be up front!”

“Fine, I’ll call and make the final arrangements as well.”

“You have another five minutes,” she said as I stood to leave.

“Thanks, use it wisely,” I said as I paid the waitress. “It’s worth nearly a hundred dollars!”

“Just asking…”

*****

Forget about the money and all the arrangements, let me tell you how Cynthia and I got on at the opera. It's the important bit really…

I was already in the car when we stopped on Third Avenue to pick up my perfect date for the night. There was no problem picking her out of the crowd! A fur coat that fell in waves from her shoulders and a small black patent bag. In the other hand was a short crop, the sort that is braided leather and has a loop for the wrist.

Keep notes, it becomes important!

She slid into the car and brought a whiff of expensive perfume with into the interior with her. The fur coat was long, it almost reached to the arches of her knitting-needle thin stiletto boots, but it did not hide the red dress below.

"Can I see?" I asked.

"Of course not! Everything is always revealed at the correct time in my world and of course I decide what the right time is. That means you follow my lead and behave yourself. There is no way that I want to ruin my reputation for utter ruthlessness by having you behave at all independently!"

I sat back in the limo and admired her as she put the finishing touches to her makeup. Eyelashes inches long with a hint of peacock blue fluttered as she checked them and then slowly applied her lipstick with a tiny paint brush. Blue, almost so deep that it was navy, applied with a coal edge that turned her lips into oracles of lust.

She tossed brush and colour into the side pocket of the car door and admired the look in the mirror.

"You won't be the only client of mine at the opera. You will just be the one who is paying at this moment," she commented. "I have to look perfect; they have to be jealous and needy. They have to come in their pants while their pathetic wives sneer without realising that I've had all their precious cocks pulsing in my rough gloved hands. That's the way that it works… You will be the only client there that has never been sexually twisted by me though. Interesting! It is a challenge I suppose."

"You look perfect," I said, "I won't say another word."

She gave me a slightly approving look and then gazed out of the window with a haughtiness that was such a turn-on that I started to understand why men paid her so much money to be mistreated.

*****

Cynthia had done her homework.

She clearly knew who Florence was and cut her out as if she had not a clue. It was a perfect snub! She cut a perfect figure of pure sexuality. That red dress, matt latex that appeared seamless. It moulded her body and rounded breasts perfectly and then trailed to a tube that fluttered around her booted ankles and made her take tiny steps on those needle heels. The crop in one hand, the Louis Vuitton bag was in the other. The smooth rippling of that fur, the fingerless gloves that allowed her manicured nails to hook like claws as she used them like a comb to adjust the black ringlets that she had assumed for the evening.

Florence watched agog as we swept to the box for eight that I had booked. My brother, looking as disreputable as ever in a slightly creased black suit, watched Cynthia with a gaze that bordered on 'agog'. When he noticed the thin silver chains that went from her ankles to somewhere up her long dress and the padlocks that sealed the boots closed I got the distinct impression that he was about to come in his pants. It was well worth the thirty grand just to see him gawp!

We arrived at the box in the Grand Tier. The tickets were for the rear row, but when Cynthia twitched her crop at the man sitting in the middle of the row, he stood and allowed us to take his seats without murmur.

I *suppose* that he was one of her 'clients', but I never dared ask her…

So we sat at the front and Aida rolled along its familiar course. Cynthia never took her eyes from the stage, she just sat so still she could have been a waxwork and I watched her for longer than I watched the action on the stage.

Already she had me in her grip. There's no doubt about it at all. Things happened later that placed me in her hand, but that night was the leap of faith that almost had me on my knees.

She was perfection.

I was obsessed.

Breasts that would have seemed moderate on an average sized woman seemed large and generous on her petite frame.

The long flowing dress and coat gave the impression that she was taller, the spiked heels made her feet almost vertical and the elaborate laces on those boots closed them in to show slender ankles and shapely calves.

More than all of that were the small touches that added meaning to her ensemble. The tiny padlocks on the boots, those tantalizing chains and the way that the matt latex moulded over her figure like a second skin.

The intermission break arrived and we headed for the bar.

I had never had people give way to me like they did that night. It was if she was the long awaited prophet parting the waters. Of course there were frowns of disapproval and whispers of disapprobation, but then there were stares of need, lust and envy that made me bathe in their light and enjoy every moment of her presence.

In the background I saw one or two people that I knew but it seemed now as if they were too shy to approach me and my new companion. I was a showpiece, a man who had somehow found the perfect woman, a woman that divided opinion and created a whisper of whispered comments from behind hands that covered lips.

The third act, the dances and the dénouement when Aida is told falsely that her lover has been killed in battle, set an emotional scene that seemed to match the still, uncanny magnificence of the woman who sat motionless and superior beside me with her blue pursed lips and long fluttering eyelashes.

Did she know then that I was falling in love with her?

Did she know that I would fall at her feet if she wanted?

Did she know that she was irresistible to me?

Of course… she was Cynthia and I was *only* a man!

How could it be otherwise?

*****

After every event, show or of course opera there is the post-event gathering. Be it in a restaurant or perhaps at the venue itself, this is the chance that all and sundry have of flaunting whatever it is that they feel the need to flaunt. After Aida, it was off to the huge bar and restaurant that the Metropolitan offers between those organic stairways that flow down the interior of the building.

Cynthia said just a few muted words of greeting as we entered the area where a buffet had been laid out. She did that which she could do so well. She made the men gaze with lust at her outré perfection and the woman sneer even though they knew that they could match neither her style nor her look. The small crop in her hand, the short tip-toe steps and her short height all created a confused picture of *what* she was, never mind what role she had in my life.

Florence entered the room and sized up her opposition. It was clear that she could not compete in looks, in style or sexual magnetism, but she was not a woman to give up easily! She strolled up to us as though it was merely casual chance at work. A slight coincidence that she just happened to join our small group.

“Hi there Ray, I don’t think that I’ve met your new girlfriend!”

“This is Cynthia,” I said with a small twinge.

This was the moment that I had paid for, this was the moment when Cynthia would *have* to deliver and I prayed that she could seize the initiative with both hands and wring Florence’s scrawny neck like a chicken.

Florence looked down at the doll-like woman and smiled. If she could not best her in the field of erotic attractiveness she was the one that could pick the battle ground. The advantage of the high ground of culture of course. We are talking about Florence, the woman who pretends such a deep awareness of the arts.

She chose the opera itself, a disarming opening…

"So what did you think of this Aida?" was her opener.

"Enjoyable…"

Cynthia's reply was almost muted and I could see Florence relax as though she thought that she had the measure of her opponent, now all she had to do was expose this doll for the empty-headed arm-candy that she was. Then she could at least claim a vast moral victory over my rejection of her when she had suggested that I attend the performance of Aida in the first place.

"I meant this actual presentation of the character of Aida in comparison to previous interpretations?" she said, Florence was coming in for the kill! "Would you say that she is up there with Leontyne Nelli or perhaps Herva Price?"

Cynthia looked pensive as if she was considering her answer and all those who were pretending not to be paying attention to the spat held their collective breath. Was this a subtle trap? The small audience that had gathered around us waited with prurient interest as they watched the two women square up…

With a casual flick of the short crop in her hand, Cynthia replied.

"Darling," she said ironically, "*Herva* Nelli and *Leontyne* Price," she said, placing the emphasis on the Christian names. "I think that you are a little confused, but I would say that for sheer atmospheric ambiance, the performance at Masada three years ago was the best that I have ever seen. In terms of the interpretation of Aida herself, Callas aside of course, I would say that Montserrat Caballé was the finest emotional performance."

There was a moment's silence and Florence fought not to blush.

She failed and a flush spread from décolletage to neck before diffusing to her cheeks.

There was no ready riposte on Florence's tongue and the best that she could manage in front of her audience was a small nod of agreement, a choked back comment and a retreat into the shadows.

The crop flickered as though punishing Florence for her temerity in trying to match wits with Cynthia. She just looked up at me with the hint of a smile on her blue lips as if to question how it was that I had ever been so foolish as to marry such an ignorant woman.

I put my arm around Cynthia's and felt her narrow waist and realised that she was wearing a corset under that smooth integument.

She was perfect…

*****

I parted from Cynthia that evening and paid her dues with a feeling that I had negotiated a bargain. Cheap at the price! But, during the next week or two I just could not get her out of my head.

I felt that I had to meet her again.

I had to have her…

*****

A week in the Hamptons up at the end of Long Island left me alone to wrestle with my feelings and I realised that my impressions of Cynthia were garbled with ideas of plans to find an excuse to meet her again.

As if I needed an excuse!

My small 'villa' up there is a refuge that I go to whenever I feel a need for solitude. I live the life of a recluse, a little fishing, mornings walking on the long beaches where the sand rustles like smoke over the periphery between land water and sky. With Cynthia, my new obsession filling my mind, I did not feel at ease at all and hardly slept but lay awake thinking of her…

One morning, after around five days there I checked my phone for the first time since arriving and found a cryptic message that simply said 'meet me'. Somehow I knew it was Cynthia. I sat for hours watching the surf batter the dunes while I tried to decide what could the correct reply.

Not too much enthusiasm, not too much eagerness, but compelling an answer.

At the end of all these ruminations I answered, 'Where?'

The next day, when I awoke, I checked my pone and found her answer '40.92003,-72.663853'. It was, of course, the latitude and longitude of the place to meet, so I texted back, 'When?'

It took just five minutes for the answer from her to come back,

‘Now!’

*****

Riverhead is a small nondescript town just an hour’s drive from my villa. I was there in forty minutes and wondered if I had the right place. The town did not seem to match my idea of the sort of place where Cynthia could possibly be interested in or even have business. I parked the pickup in a nearby shopping car park and wandered towards the railway crossing. All the while I was scanning for her small figure and trying to imagine what game she was playing.

As I stood rather nonplussed by the bleak roadside a long limousine pulled up beside me and the window rolled down.

“Ray Lever?” said the woman who sat in the shadows of the car.

“Erm, yes,” I replied.

“I have been sent to pick you up!”

The rear door opened and I saw an invitingly deep clad leather nest, empty of occupants. I slid into the space and the door closed automatically and I found myself being transported who knew where.

The windows were dark and it was difficult to see where we were going, not that I knew this part of the island well at all anyway.

The driver did not speak; she sat behind her closed window and smoothly drove to the mystery rendezvous. It took an hour and a half, during which I tried to imagine all the things that might happen at the place where I was going. After a while I started to enjoy the mystery of the situation and relaxed a little into the spirit of the jaunt. This so fitted Cynthia, doubt and hope and an enigma!

I explored the interior of the car and found a small fridge, well stocked with Champagne and spirits, as well as several holes concealed in the luxurious leather from which peeped padlocks on chains. Strange! I could not imagine a use for them, but the Whiskey distracted me and I poured myself a glass and sat sipping as the countryside rolled by like a stately movie.

At long last the limousine pulled up at a high security gate, paused a moment and then rolled into a broad expanse of grass and solitary trees before pulling up before a huge house, a stately home really, that hinted at old money, perhaps even wealth beyond my own.

The door opened and I found myself being led by the attractive driver to a massive front door which opened slowly as we approached. Standing inside was Cynthia, dressed in a summer frock and high heeled sandals. In her hand was the ever-present crop which now seemed at odds with the bright summer colours of her silk dress.

"I found out that you were in the neighbourhood," said Cynthia, "and I thought that you might fancy an afternoon of relaxed intelligent conversation."

"Is this your house?"

Cynthia laughed, "No it belongs to a dear friend of mine, but I have a key and occasionally use it to escape the hurly-burley of New York."

She led me through the hallway to the right into a gorgeous red room that was filled with heavy and rich furniture and had a fire burning in the grate.

"Your friend must really be quite wealthy," I commented as we sat and Cynthia pulled at a small hanging handle that swung from a fine chain. "And naturally a person of excellent taste!"

"I have to agree," said Cynthia. "Refined taste, as she would say. It could well be that she is even more wealthy than you, Ray, but she does not choose to live in a small villa on the bleak coast like you do!"

"Ah," I answered, "you have been doing a little research…"

"Of course, it is vital to get these things correct, to know what is what and who is who. I like to know the people that I associate with intimately."

"Like when we watched Aida?"

"Exactly. I watched the whole performance at Masada on video from one end to the other, even though opera bores me *intensely*."

"It does me," I replied, "I have to admit that I just wanted to see the confrontation after the performance. In fact *your* performance was so much more perfectly studied than even Maria Callas and all those others that you mentioned!"

"The incident was amusing," she smiled, "in fact enjoyable! So much so that I thought that you might be of some interest to me and that we should perhaps meet again."

"Am I paying for this pleasure?"

"Of course! There is always a price to pay, as you will discover. It's just that it does not always have to be money, sometimes the price is costs even more than that!"

I wanted to follow up her comment, but at that moment a maid appeared and stood to wait by the door.

"What would you like?" she asked. "Tea, perhaps coffee or something stronger? A bite to eat… do you have a preference?"

"I had Bourbon in the car," I replied. "Tea is fine and a few cakes or something light like that, perhaps?"

Cynthia turned to the maid and nodded.

"I will have the same," she said.

The maid turned on her heels and went to fetch and I realised that I had forgotten what I had been about to say before the maid arrived.

"Your friend, the one that owns this mansion, does she have a name?" I asked.

"Irene," replied Cynthia. "She is here somewhere so she may be down later. At the moment she is very busy… I'm sure that she'll make the time to look in. She has an interest in men…"

I imagined a young businesswoman and wondered how she came to know Cynthia, a woman from the shadowed sinful side of the tracks.

"What does she do?" I asked to fill the silence.

"Mainly educational work, but I suppose that you could say that she teaches people of all walks of life what it is that they were born for!"

"Intriguing," I said.

"She is!"

There was a short silence and I looked around the room. I have not all that much idea of art, but it was clear that the contents of this room represented hundreds of thousands of dollars and that the furniture was not just luxurious, but antique as well.

"I invited you here to make to get to know you better," said Cynthia.

I settled back and wondered what this was about, but at that moment the maid reappeared with a tray stacked with all the accoutrements for making afternoon tea in the old fashioned way. She approached the low table that lay between Cynthia and myself with small steps and I glanced up at her and found myself smitten by what I saw. She was a pretty young woman, shapely hips, rounded ass and long legs topped off with narrow waist, plentiful breasts and a severe but attractive face. The mansions of America are full of servants, uniformed and gracious, that is not at all unusual. Old money still needs service. What caught my breath was that she was dressed in a uniform that at a distance might have been taken for typical 'French maid'. Close up she was so much more and less. Less because the uniform scarcely concealed her charms, they lay *just* out of view. More, because she moved in small steps because a slender chain hung between her well-turned ankles and her feet were locked into her stilettos. Her hands wore thin bracelets with small padlocks that hung loose and a collar on her neck displayed a slight hint of a green light that blinked as she served us the tea.

“Do you like her?” asked Cynthia with one eyebrow raised.

“She is attractive,” I stuttered.

“If you want to use her, then she is yours!”

I looked into Cynthia’s eyes and saw that she was serious. As she spoke the small crop in her hand lifted the hen of the maid’s dress to show a perfectly smooth ass that was tattooed with a delicate pattern of roses growing from between her thighs to bloom on that silky skin.

The maid ignored the attention and poured before standing still and waiting for further orders.

“You may now fetch the food,” said Cynthia to her as she lowered the crop.

The maid stepped and left the room with perfect steps that caused her hips to tilt at each step and click the metal heels of her stilettos on the hard wood floor.

“What did you mean by, ‘If you want to use her, then she is yours’?” I asked.

“She’s only a maid,” said Cynthia as she reached for her teacup. “They are here to please all of the owners and guests that use this house of Irene’s. I occasionally avail myself…”

I was shocked. I knew that Cynthia was a dominatrix by choice, that she must probably enjoy making men squirm, but I had the seemingly unreasonable idea that somehow that was just her job and that she would be different in ‘real life’.

The maid returned with a tray full of small cakes and savouries and laid them on the table.

“Do you enjoy working here?” asked Cynthia of her as she worked.

“Yes Ma’am,” she replied.

“”My friend here,” Cynthia pointed at me with the tip of her crop, “would like you to pleasure him now… He would like you to show him how skilled you are!”

The maid placed her plates on the table and slowly lowered to her knees. With a small movement she moved forward to come between my legs. I looked at Cynthia and did not know how to react. This was not what I had come for, it was Cynthia that I had imagined between my legs and not some substitute, no matter how attractive. That did not stop me feeling a strong erection pressing against my pants!

The maid’s hand’s reached for me and I moved to stop her.

“Just enjoy, don’t be so shy,” said Cynthia with a small smile. “She is exceptionally good with lips and tongue! I always ask for her when I am here!”

I moved my hands and the maid delicately opened my pants to allow my cock to push its way into the light. Her hands closed on me and her lips pursed. The expression on her face was pure concentration and absorption in her task as she slowly pulled me back to expose the head of my cock.

Lips pursed and her tongue licked me with an almost tender flick.

I gasped and watched Cynthia sit back to enjoy the little show that she had initiated. In one hand was her ever present crop; in the other was her tea cup as she delicately sipped the hot Jasmine tea with small sips.

The maid lowered and her lips slowly descended over my cock.

I could feel her tongue work at me, tickling the tip, the ridge and vein and then sucking me in further than I had ever been in a woman's mouth. As I watched the lips went ever further and I felt myself being drawn into her throat. I saw my cock make her throat bulge as her lips finally reached my balls and her tongue slipped out to massage them as she choked on my rigid cock.

I gasped, the feeling was utterly exhilarating as the maid moved to slide me in and out with an irregular rhythm. It excited and brought me close, but did not threaten to make me climax. All the while Cynthia watched me and smiled. I could see a slight flush spread over her neck and face as she relished the entertainment and sipped her tea.

The small crop tapped her thigh, but there was no other response from Cynthia.

A minute? Five? Who knows? I ascended and descended until I was almost frantic to come, but I could not utter the words, speak the order and the maid just kept me at a point short of the peak while Cynthia licked her lips.

Finally the crop moved.

It tapped the maid on her ass and signaled that Cynthia expected something from her.

The irregular rhythm was replaced by a slow timed cadence that was calculated to milk me in short order. I gasped, she responded with a slight lessening of pressure, but I was to be emptied nevertheless.

I cried out, the pleasure was beyond all my experience.

I felt that urgent surge through my groin and balls. I knew that the inevitable was about to occur and I could not help but strain and push my hips up and make her swallow every last inch of my needy prick.

Time slowed.

I saw Cynthia sip her tea. I saw the maid's ass in the air, the hem of her dress fallen forward over her waist to expose those roses that budded on her smooth skin. The cleft of her ass. I saw the room, the gilt and oils, the leather and velvet. I saw a middle aged woman standing framed in the doorway. I saw the motes of dust swirl and dance in the slanting sunbeams that shot through the windows and I saw that impatient crop tap on that silk clad knee.

Most of all I saw Cynthia.

The woman who was giving me a blow job by proxy, fellatio with another's lips and throat, irrumation by substitution. I was hooked as she caught my wild stare and held me with just the strength of her gaze as I pumped the maid full of come and gasped with the climax.

I saw the maid lift her head and kiss the last few drops from me before she slid the zipper on my pants and buried my depleted cock back in its place.

The maid stood and nodded her head in a small bow and then finished laying the table that my pleasure had interrupted. It was curious, that moment that was normally full of feedback with a partner, that moment after orgasm, but the maid tripped out of the room, passing the woman who stood smiling at the entrance.

“I hope that you are satisfied with the service here,” said the woman as she stepped into the room. “We punish poor service severely!”

Her presence was so overwhelming that the room seemed to shrink. Dressed in severe leather skirt and white flouncy blouse, she walked on her heels as though she had been born in them.

“Irene?” I asked.

“Indeed, and you must be Ray, the man who paid my friend fifty thousand for a night’s accompaniment. I can do nothing but congratulate you in your choice. She is a rare diamond, is Cynthia.”

I felt myself blushing, but Irene simply swatted her hand a little as if dismissing the events that she had witnessed.

“I hear that you have a villa on the coast?”

“That’s right, Dune Road.”

“You will of course be staying here?” she asked.

“Erm, perhaps a single night.”

“He’s a little shy,” said Cynthia with a small titter.

"Well, shyness is certainly a novelty here," said Irene. "There's no point in having a house and servants like mine unless everyone gets to use them to the full. That's the whole point of it and I am sure that Ray would agree!"

I nodded.

It seemed…

...required.

"Well, I'll let you two love-birds alone, the last thing that you need is me here spoiling all the fun. If you need anything special, just have a word with Veronica, she's here around somewhere…"

With that Irene walked from the room. She might have been well over fifty, but she had a forceful brand of sexual attractiveness that left the room empty when she exited despite the fact that the centre of my obsession sat facing me.

"Love-birds?" I asked.

"I let something slip to Irene earlier, but let's not discuss that now. We'll have a bite to eat, drink a little civilised tea and get to know one another."

"Sounds fine."

*****

It was outlandish, a discussion with the woman who was my obsession just after she had watched me being fellated by what seemed to be a willing slave who was at her beck and call. As for Irene, who ran the establishment, well, I was at a loss for words.

Small talk, inconsequential chatter about the night at the opera, me telling her about my previous marriages, her hinting at her own profession and telling me again that she never allowed the clients to have intercourse, though what this said about all the other sexual possibilities, I could not divine. The plates were taken by the same maid and I suddenly felt tempted to tease.

"Maid!" I asked in a stern voice. "What is your name?"

She stood straight and replied, "Thirty Six!"

I was nonplussed by this answer and it stopped me asking her if she fancied meeting up with me sometime.

"They are all just numbered," said Cynthia. "The odd numbered ones are females and the even numbered ones are man-sluts."

"Thirty six," I muttered as though unable to calculate.

Cynthia doubled up with laughter at my confusion and then said, "Show him, Thirty Six!"

The maid lifted the hem of her skirt and showed me the bare midriff, smooth and hairless it angled down to a tiny dangling cock and grape-like balls. A ring pierced the tip of the cock and a chain hung from it to be locked onto a steel bracelet that circled those tiny balls. A green light flickered on that steel like it did on the collar at her neck.

I could not think of the maid as male, in my head she was female, despite what I had seen!

"He used to be one of my clients…" said Cynthia. "If I remember correctly he was running a small chain of restaurants when he met me. Irene is so greedy really, I'm not sure that I approve of her methods, but they certainly work!"

"Is she here voluntarily, I mean does she want to be here, in this… Erm, house?"

I wanted to say 'brothel', but the word failed me at the last moment.

"Ask her, then!"

"Thirty Six, are you here willingly? Serving…"

"I live to serve Miss Irene and Miss Cynthia," she said.

"I'm afraid that's all the answer that you are going to get," said Cynthia as she dismissed the maid with a slight movement of the hand. "There are some men who just fall and fall; I meet them all the time."

"Are you suggesting that…?"

"What? That you are here to end your days as a slutty cock sucking sissy-maid? Actually, it's up to you! I'm not that sure that you have the figure for it!"

The whole idea of Cynthia having tricked me and having sucked off by some transvestite, she-male or whatever made me more than uneasy. I started to get the feeling that my obsession with this woman was really dangerous ground. I'm not at all a prude, quite the opposite, but this was stretching the description of 'tea in the afternoon' to the absolute limit. I didn't know how to take all of this and decided to change the subject to something more comfortable.

“Can I see the rest of the house?”

“The bits that are not private,” she answered

So we took a walk around the house.

I did not see numbers One to Thirty Five in evidence and wondered if there was just one maid in the whole place. The rooms were elegant and luxurious, the facilities well organised and the house was in fact seemingly empty.

Cynthia and I were looking out of a window over the grounds and I asked what all the blocks were around the front and rear of the house.

“That’s Irene’s Institute,” said Cynthia. “It’s off-limits… at the moment. She just had it rebuilt.”

She turned to survey the room and said, “This can be your room for the night. The bathroom is here,” she waved a hand, “and you can lock the door. If you lock the door, nothing will happen. If you leave it unlocked, anything could happen…”

I raised an eyebrow and said, “Does the ‘anything’ include you?”

“Would you like it to?”

“Very much.”

We’ll see.”

*****

I was the only man that I saw in the house, well, apart from that maid anyway. We had a rather formal meal and then retired to a salon that was fitted as a cinema with plush leather sofas and Chesterfield chairs. The latest film played on the big screen and I sat next to Cynthia glancing occasionally at her rapt face as she was absorbed by the story.

Sitting with us were three women and Irene. Veronica, a silent rather stiff woman who was the only one to dress casually. Hillary, a youngish woman who seemed in some way to be Veronica's partner and finally an attractive lawyer from Miami called Crystal. There was not much conversation and not just a few curious glances at my intrusive presence. It seemed, however, that Irene's word was law, because she initiated every conversation, suggested the food, ordered the drinks and decided what film we were to watch without demur.

At last the night drew to a close and I headed for my room.

A maid passed me.

"What number are you?" I asked.

"Ten," she said as she turned to face me.

She had unnaturally large breasts and wide hips with shapely legs and a waist that looked as if it would snap. Her dress was so tight that I could see the tight corset and the straps that held up her stockings.

Or do I mean his stockings?

I get so confused that I shall go from appearances!

"Show me!" I ordered.

Ten lifted her skirt and showed me that, indeed she was male, or had been. I stepped forward and reached for the collar that flashed with a small green light, but as I did, Irene came around the corner and suddenly I felt like a guilty child who was touching something that they shouldn't.

She raised an eyebrow and smiled.

"Ten is a perfect slut," she said. "If you want her for the night… She has a thousand tricks up her sleeve and in a few other places as well."

"Erm, no thanks," I managed to say as I retreated to my room.

For a minute I leaned on the back of the door and breathed until at last my heart had slowed. This house was a terrible or beautiful place. Perhaps it was both? My problem was that I lack a moral compass and have no idea what is right and wrong. At least that's what Florence always said.

I turned and looked at the key in the door.

Should I lock the door or not?

That was the question, the question that crazed my judgement.

*****

Of course I hear you say, '*Lock the door fool, hide in the room, escape with the cold light of the dawning sun and never look back over your shoulder!*'

I could not; I cannot save myself from myself. It would be a betrayal of *me*, a betrayal of my own character and that I cannot do, it is one of my most basic characteristics. This 'not being able to control my circumstances'. It's how I came to marry Florence after all!

*****

I took the key and without locking the door, placed it carefully on the door handle so that when the door was opened it would drop on the floor and wake me. That was my precaution… Not to stop what was about to happen, but to forewarn myself of its actually happening!

I switched off the light and found myself in utter darkness. Sometimes, after being blinded by light, twenty minutes later the eye can pick surface and shape from the clawing dark. This room was so dark that the gloom was absolute and there was nothing to break the cloak that descended. I fumbled my way to the bed and slipped in between the coverlets to feel the fresh sheets pull at my skin with that delicious coolness that is matched by the unique flow of pure linen.

I thought that I would never manage to slip into sleep.

Thoughts of Cynthia filled my head.

I decided that she would visit.

A fuck was coming.

With Cynthia.

A fuck!

*****

The key dropped onto the hard wood of the floor by the door and I awoke. I heard the door open slowly. It did not creak; it did not moan or rasp, there was a slight click and the slight sound of the air displaced by wood.

The corridor beyond was in darkness and I felt rather than heard the woman who entered my room with a slight click of heel and a faint tick as the door closed behind her. I could not see her, but I could perceive her breathing, I heard a slight creak as if leather, a rustle as thighs crossed and lace rubbed.

It seemed to take an age for her to reach my bed, an eon before her hand laid on my shoulder lightly.

“I have decided,” she whispered from the shadows.

It was Cynthia.

“What have you decided?” I asked.

“Soon I shall tell you, my dear, but first…”

I felt the nails scratch as she pulled back the sheet. They ran in stripes down my arms as the cool air of the room displaced the warm air under the sheet. The cover was pulled free of my nakedness, it dropped with a murmur, a sigh and then the hands were gone.

I shivered, not with the exposure to the cool air, but in anticipation of her touch again.

I could feel my blood rising and wondered how making love to this exquisite women would be different from all the other women that had been on the end my cock…

I knew that she was a sadist; I knew that she had to be in control, I knew that she had a single minded intelligence that would surely overwhelm me, but I just had to taste the poison.

The hand drifted lightly from my groin to lips, flicking the nails to score me to anticipation of pleasure. My prick hardened, stood and sought solace, but her hands were busy investigating and tantalizing and did not offer comfort. My hips thrust a little and I heard a low chuckle from Cynthia as if she were pleased that I responded so well at her light touch.

The hands moved south.

I thrust, I could not help myself.

"Always *my* pleasure foremost, that is the first lesson," she whispered.

I felt her join me on the bed. I felt that hard leather of her boots. The spikes caught me and scraped my calves with their needle points. Then the rasp of the laces, the scraping of the hooks and metal eyelets on his thighs as she sat astride me. Pinning me to the bed.

I could feel my cock graze something rough and hard as she leaned forward. Her heels dug into my calves and I struggled not to raise my hands and lift her slight figure and sit her firmly on my jutting and hungry prick. She moved, I felt my cock being pushed and then it slid between her thighs to find and pass between the lips of her sweet, sweet cunt. Not inside, no, she rubbed herself along the length of me. My prick was the object that she would pleasure herself on! I was her pleasure seat, her vibrator, merely an object that she could use to satisfy her need!

Her clit rubbed on my shaft, the lower edge of her corset gouged the tip of my cock and her slim fingers held me firmly to keep me in place. A slight moan, that was all that I heard from her, a sigh that moved to a lower register as she climaxed on me, using me, rubbing herself and playing the superior.

Playing? This was no game!

I felt myself moving towards climax, but I knew that that was not in the unspoken rules. Her rules, the law of Cynthia. If I wanted to come, if I wanted to fuck, then it had to be when *she* allowed it. It had to be on *her* terms.

So I lay still while I felt her tremble and come with a slight clench of thighs and a ragged breath, I sensed her pussy dripping oil onto my prick, smoothing through the outer portals of her cunt. That corset punished the tip of my cock, but my mind begged for more.

Again.

I felt the light touch of the crop on my lips and kissed it while she climaxed again in a long trembling shudder. Her thighs gripped me and she was still. I remember praying that she would allow me… that she would permit me to enter, that she needed me as much as I needed her.

Her thighs tightened and she lifted.

I felt a hand guide me upright.

The tip of me ploughed her from the front; it opened her slick cunt and finally poised at the brink of the heaven that I was risking so much for.

Poised before the gates, her nails scratching me, guiding me into her depths, it was a moment of stasis that left me holding my breath when her whispered voice came from the darkness.

"Will you be mine?" she asked.

How could I do other at this moment as I stood on the edge of a cliff and looked down at the fantastic valley below?

How could I do other than jump?

"Please!"

"Is that a promise?"

"Yes, it's a promise."

"Will you marry me, my little bitch?"

I heard the proposal, the words flickered through my head, I imagined her sliding down on me, taking me in, sucking me dry. Milking me in her exquisite body, forcing me to jump over that cliff and flutter like a butterfly to the fields below.

"Please, Cynthia, I will."

Those words triggered the long awaited fall. She spread her thighs and slipped slowly over me, swallowing me into her, sucking me in and holding me tight. It took so long; I was almost demented by the time that the delicate lips of her pussy pressed against the root of my cock. A short trip, but one that took forever! It was all I had hoped, heaven as she rested and then slowly rose to suck and pull at me. It was as if I were enclosed in a gentle tight fist, a mouth that knew my every nerve, a place where I fitted to perfection.

I sighed and she leaned forward, placing her hands on my chest as she rose and fell, tearing me from her, impaling herself on me, controlling and timing the fuck to make perfection as she climaxed again and again with small shivers that made the fuck ever more delicious. Poignant and exquisite.

I moved my hands, raised them to touch her face, but her own hands moved to press my wrists down and then I was coming. Climaxing, desperation, short breaths and then a moan when the pace changed and I was held on the brink of that chasm for a few seconds before she allowed me to climax.

I have never had it like that before.

Never been so guided and led.

I almost fainted as I felt myself spurt into her, spray as if it were the first and only time.

I was deep inside and Cynthia was still.

"Will you still marry me?" she asked.

"Cynthia, darling I will marry you!"

"Are you mine to do with as I wish?"

"I am."

"To have and to hold?"

"Will you love and obey?"

"I will."

She sat back and I felt her hand move to prevent me slipping from her and then the light went on! I had a momentary sight of her in black and then I had to close my eyes from the brightness that Cynthia had created.

I heard a small laugh and then I slowly opened my eyes to look up at the woman who had proposed and bought me with a perfect fuck. A fuck in the dark that had been such perfect mixture between pleasure pure and pain.

She stood over me and looked down and I opened my eyes to gaze at the woman who was to be my next wife. I saw the corset. It was laced fantastically tight, painfully constricting her to make a wasp of her. It swelled her hips and lifted those breasts high to tumble over the confines of that leather with small chains hanging from the pierced nipples. The smooth neck, the silver collar and then finally the smooth masked face whose lips were savagely forced apart by a huge ball that left her face with surprise at being orally raped by nothing more than a rubber ball.

Eyes smooth, nose smooth, ears and hair smoothed away, just the red circle of the gag and the collar that I had seen in more than one neck in Irene's sexual playground. I had fucked another of the submissive denizens of Irene's mansion.

I gasped and looked to the left where Cynthia stood in her summer dress with her crop in her hand. A smile turned the corners of her mouth slightly and the tip of the crop touched my lips.

Enjoining me to silence.

Planted on my prick was her substitute, a rubber dolly, a silent helpless fuck that had been the flesh to go with Cynthia's whispering voice in the utter dark.

"She is me too," said Cynthia. "She is my cunt, my breasts, my body when I want her to be. She is the perfect rubber dolly in the dark, made more lovable by her absolute helplessness. Made more attractive by a cruel training that makes her better than any toy and more obedient than any bitch."

The tip of the crop rested and I pouted slightly as she noticed and smiled.

"You will be a perfect husband for me, Ray," she said. "I will tease you and then empty you as and when I want. You will love me, look after me and make me happy. A perfect marriage…"

"Cynthia, I do not know if I am in the grip of obsession or love," I said through the braids of her crop.

"Both?" she suggested.

"Both!"

*****

I was almost glad to leave Irene's little sexual palace of torment behind and glad not to see *her* again.

Cynthia is frightening, there is no doubt about that in my mind.

But Irene is terrifying.

It is she who collars her slaves and compels them to service.

It is she who organizes training with invisible bars and locks as they pass from one electronically and computer-controlled zone to the next.

Their lights shine green when they are safe from punishment, flashing green signifies warning and red means that the computer will punish and torment them as Irene programmed.

I no longer believe that the 'maids' are anything other than sexual chattels, slaves to lust, degenerate and destroyed men and women who have fallen into the clutches of a woman who knows no shred of humanity. Only her blissful pleasure as she controls their lives, their every breath and their every thought is of concern to her.

That and the deadly place between her thighs.

Cynthia, the woman that I lust for, the obsession that I love, the passion who knows how to push me further and further down a path of her choosing… Cynthia could *never* be like Irene, she is pure! An angel of torment and not a demon of pain.

Of this I am sure!

*****

There was so much to do.

A wedding, my funeral, was not easily arranged in the short time that she suggested as a frame for its organization. I had to do it all, the arrangements, the invitations, the costs, the flowers, cars, cake, Champagne. The only things that she organised were the things that she personally wanted to attend to. I did all the rest!

A visit by her attorney to draw up the arrangement was next.

Attorney at law, Mr Gregory Howard was a quiet man who seemed almost out of place in his suit.

In his hand was a briefcase with all of the papers prepared and ready to sign.

I thought that he looked anxious, but that might just have been my imagination.

"It's all just a standard contract, just as ordered," he said. "The only sum guaranteed to Cynthia is a simple million, which she gets in every case. She cannot receive more unless Mr Lever decides to be generous. I have tied this to a will for him to sign as well. This will be administered by a trust fund. Trustees to be nominated by Mr Lever of course. That fund is only for use in the case of his death or being mentally debilitated so that he is not legally able to make decisions about his future."

Cynthia passed the file to me and I read it through. There was no doubt that Mr Howard had drawn up a pretty thorough document. In fact it looked almost word for word the same as the one that I had signed when I had married Florence. The only difference was that Florence's lawyer had written ten million dollars and Cynthia's had written just a million. I would have offered more, but I was sure that Cynthia had instructed him and that she would just ignore any changes in that direction.

"By all means take a copy to your lawyer and have it checked through," he said with a small smile. "As soon as you are satisfied, then just sign it here and I'll get my secretary to witness it. It becomes 'in force' the moment that you are man and wife and not before!"

Cynthia waved that crop of hers, tapped it on the page and I knew that she wanted me to sign now. It would show approval of her choice of attorney, it would show faith in her and most of all it was just what *she* wanted.

I signed and Mr Howard called in his secretary to witness the document.

"I'll have it notarised and a copy made for your records, Mr Lever," he said. "So, all that is left to me is to wish you happiness and success in the coming years…"

I thanked him and that was that.

The next visit was to organise the ceremony and all that would fit around the church service. We wrote the vows together and she decided where the guests would sit.

All of this passed by so quickly.

She organised her life and set up our new home in a small mansion just up at Sand's Point. Not close enough to be called 'New York'. Not far enough away to make access difficult, being just forty minutes to Manhattan. She got the builders in and rebuilt the whole house for just a few hundred thousand.

"I am not going to waste your money, darling," was her only comment, but she would not let me see it until the wedding, her little present!

*****

Now, I know what you are thinking. What happened before the wedding? Did our hero fuck his wife-to-be? Did she just find another replacement for her own full blooded participation? What happened to the sex-slave who did so much to milk the agreement from me to marry?

I'll answer all those questions.

But one at a time and at my own pace!

Despite throwing money around, despite me hiring organizers and others, the whole wedding took two months to organise and then another month waiting. On the other hand, I suppose that three months for a 'society' wedding with all the trimmings as well as a rebuild of a grand old house is not *too* long.

During this time I spent time between my Long Island villa and New York as I organised and got organised. In New York we went to restaurants, we dined and went to shows and parties. Cinema and Central Park. Chocolate strawberries from Godiva on 7th Avenue and the balcony on the top of the Empire State where she allowed *me* to propose to *her* and she accepted, closing the circle.

A 'regular' romance unbroken by any sexual contact between us.

It was unsullied and pure!

Then there was the dark romance that we carried on in the shadow of the first. A place where we went, led naturally by Cynthia, a walk in the darkness of fetishism and almost-madness. Cynthia took my hand and led me slowly down the path to sex without love, sex without mercy, sex without romance, sex without gentleness, sex without compassion, and most of all, avaricious sex without moral guilt.

In my small villa, a cage in the cellar held the woman whose name was Three, whom Irene lent to Cynthia with a casual flick of her manicured finger. That woman was used as out tool, our substitute for Cynthia, because she would not allow me to touch her in the dark of the bedroom.

A surly middle-aged matron came along with the slave, a large breasted barrel of a woman who ensured that the bitch in the cage was kept fit for use as we needed. It guaranteed that privacy was total and the escape of our unwilling helper was impossible.

Now that I look back, I see how far and fast I had fallen. I had allowed myself to be inched between Cynthia's thighs, never to touch her pussy, never to taste the wine of her ass or the smooth taut flesh that smoothed her breasts. And yet, I was permitted all that, and more, of the muted figure who we played with every night that we spent at my villa on Long Island.

*****

One night, after three days in New York, I met with Cynthia at the villa. Now there was but a week to the wedding. When she would become my wife and I her husband. I was standing on the porch looking over the grey Atlantic rollers as her car arrived and she stepped, immaculate as always, onto the porch.

"I love the wild wind that howls through here in the winter," she said.

"That's why I bought the place," I replied. "The sand skips the beach like a layer of a frailer reality…"

"You can get quite poetic," she laughed looking up at me.

"I do have just a little poetry in my soul, actually!"

"I know you do Raymond," she replied.

The wind started to blow and she pulled her fur coat a little closer to her body in response and pulled up the collar high. I looked down and longed to kiss her, to lean down and receive a reward for my imagination. Her lips pursed and then straightened and she looked over the beach.

"A heaped fire, a bottle of brandy, our willing little slut and you… I think that this last evening together will be perfect for us!"

"Last evening?"

"Well, we are married in a week and then we will be together so much more. I have to be in New York tomorrow to meet some special people. I have arranged a little honeymoon in San Francisco for us. I found a delightful hotel in a place called Ocean Cove. Private and a perfect place to get to know each other so much more intimately. We'll go out there a week after the wedding and find each other!"

Cynthia led the way into the house.

Dinner was a slow affair, as usual I wanted to hurry, to get to find out what Cynthia had in mind for our amusement, but she did what she always did. She took her time and showed in yet another way how much she was in control of both of us.

We sipped the cognac, we listened to and commented on the howling gale that was building up outside. We relished our coffees and stared at the flames as my erection threatened to split my pants and thrust into the firelight.

At last Cynthia called in that middle aged guardian of our slave. A veritable matron. She slid into the room as if staying unnoticed in shadows was her métier.

She stood impassive by the door waiting for our needs to be known. Her face was expressionless as she watched us and only when Cynthia made a small sign with her crop did she go to fetch our special unwilling human pleasure doll.

As the matron went to fetch her from her cage in the cellar, I asked, "Cynthia, where does our little 'helper' come from? I mean who was she before she was lent to us? Who was she before she became Three?"

Cynthia sighed.

"Darling if you start asking questions like that, you are on the road to ruin. All that is important *is* that she is here for *our* pleasure and nothing else. Irene has kindly lent us the single-most valuable slave that she has and you should be grateful and not question where the present comes from."

"I just wondered..."

"All that I know is that her name was Denise, but that was years ago. Before my time. Now she just is just Irene's personal body slave..."

"Oh!"

The door opened and Denise was led into the room by the maid. Collared with a leash she was a vision in black that seemed bizarrely like a shop window display dummy magically brought to life. Every detail of her body, from her feet in high heels, to the top of her head where a ponytail of black hair sprouted and fell, was on display. A shiny black integument that showed every contour, every move of muscle and yet deprived her of all individuality. Her face was smooth where eyes and lashes had been painted onto the latex. Her mouth pouted, but was closed by a handy zipper; Denise was lost, there was no character to be divined in this fuck-doll.

Three was a body without a soul, a shape without individuality.

The guardian matron came to a standstill and glanced at her helpless charge with a look that could have been contempt for her vulnerability or perhaps just a sneer at her low station.

"You can leave now," said Cynthia.

The matron let the loop of the leash fall gently and nodded.

"I shall be here when you call, Ma'am."

Cynthia waved her hand slightly as if brushing the woman from her mind and walked around the black figure that stood helpless and waiting for abuse.

"Tonight I have a special little game for us to play," said Cynthia as she played with the zipper that allowed access to the front and rear of the slave. "Do you want to play?"

I could not help myself, my cock was rigid with expectation and the thought that Cynthia might be more than a passive observer who simply directed *my* pleasure gave me hope that the honeymoon might just be *that* special moment when she finally allowed me to do more than make love to the substitutes that she supplied me.

"Please," I begged.

She smiled and looked at the bulge in my pants. The effect that she was having on me was stronger than it had ever been. Cynthia had created a madman of me, nurtured my obsession and fed its debauched need. Just the sight of her in charge was enough to make me shamefully depraved.

“Tonight, since it is the last night together like this before we marry; I have decided to allow you to kiss *me* while you take your pleasure.”

I felt an irrational surge of delight as though she had offered me something beyond compare and it never really was more than a phantom thought that what I was allowing was for Cynthia to condition me to her needs.

The slave waited on all fours for our attentions and Cynthia arranged things to her satisfaction as she usually did. A small slap on the mute service slave’s behind shuffled her into position facing the easy chair where Cynthia would be sitting. A tweak of the fingers and the zipper that concealed the pale milky skin under all that matt black was slowly revealed. As the zipper descended, slowly, the flesh welled and was exposed. A smooth, slightly blue veined, porcelain softness, a hairless and smooth ass that invited further investigation and use.

Cynthia glanced at me and she smiled as her hand reached the point where that pouting sex was revealed. Puckering, inviting, but almost asexual in form. A perfect cunt, white skin showing a deep pink inner life that begged to be filled. It dripped a little, that cunt, a teardrop as it cried for attention. Then the small bud of Denise’s clitoris showed and I felt myself need to take that doll from behind.

Cynthia’s hand withdrew and she allowed one nail to slide along the length of that revealed sex and then pause on the pink pucker of her asshole.

“Which do you need, darling?” she asked as she slowly settled in the chair and moved to rest her feet on the small of the kneeling slave’s back.

I could not resist. There was something so erotically charged about Cynthia's slow and cool manner. Her ruthless use of a helpless proxy. I undid my pants and looked down at the ass that I was about to fuck. It invited abuse, it was perfect and needing to be soiled. I pressed my cock against the rosebud of that ass in answer to my wife to be.

She smiled and made a small movement with her hand as if inviting me to press home and fuck my dolly. In a small pique of resistance to Cynthia I allowed the tip of my rigid cock to drop and slowly pushed home into that cunt, that perfect tunnel. I closed my eyes and imagined that I had *Cynthia* on the end of my cock; I imagined her squealing with surprise as she felt the size of me. I imagined her gasping and trying to escape as I fucked her.

I imagined…

But the slave stayed quiet and simply moved her hips a little to help me slide into her with ease. A slight wiggle and her thighs opened a little to allow me to press home as deep as possible. In her black world of night she was just a hole to be fucked, a piece of furniture that her owner would offer to whomsoever she felt fit.

I opened my eyes.

Cynthia sat at ease, her legs on the back of the woman that I was fucking in her stead. I could not see up her tight skirt except that my eyes caught a glimpse of what might have been just a little white thigh above the tops of her stockings. What I was seeing for the first time was that she was slowly unbuttoning her blouse.

The lace of her bra, her breasts bursting out of the cups, her hand slowly revealing them to me. My hips twitched as she caught my eye and I was falling into a hypnosis of need that Cynthia was feeding as she licked her lips and slid her blouse to the side to reveal what I now imagined to be the most perfect breasts that I had ever seen.

"Would you like to see more?" she asked.

I think that I just gasped and thrust into the substitute even harder as she cupped herself.

"Would you like to kiss me?" she asked.

Oh, yes please," I gasped, imagining that I was to place my lips on the nipples that were emerging as her hands released the bra that cupped her breasts.

The two halves of the bra separated. Her breasts were revealed, each with a delicate rose tattooed to make her nipples a bouquet of two perfect pink blooms. I was so close to climax, so close to coming as I stared at my wife-to-be and tried to lean to put those small nipples to my lips as she had promised, but she was well out of my reach and I could not pull from the cunt of the slave that I was filling so I just pouted as I leaned forward.

One of her feet lifted.

The shoe was presented to my lips and I kissed it in a desperate need for contact as my thighs clenched and I shot into Denise as the heels of Cynthia's stilettos pushed past my lips.

"That's good, dear. This is something that you will do for me often..."

I saw that she had slipped a hand into the waistband of her skirt, I saw the rapture on her beautiful face, I saw those breasts flush, heave with orgasm. I felt the thrust of me into the plastic flesh of the sub-human that was nothing more than a receptacle to use. I came in a gush, deep inside and slowly withdrew as the shoe moved to place the sole on my lips.

I kissed it and Cynthia gasped and came with a rush, so I kissed again and again to send her to her own heaven.

I think that it was the first time that she climaxed at my touch.

*****

It is all very well for you, the listener, to realise that my wife to be, the delectable Cynthia was doing nothing more than to condition me to her immoral personal taste. I was being groomed, trained, prepared and sucked into her sinful life as something that might *eventually* have even less value than the slave she had borrowed as a fuck toy for her lover.

I knew all of that as I kissed her shoes, I knew that I was falling, I knew that I was being tutored, but my need overcame everything. My impractical belief that progress was being made, the idea that slowly she was allowing me more. The hare-brained certain knowledge that the marriage would change everything. That in the end I would be her lover, her confidant, her partner, this was certain in my head.

*****

Before the wedding, that fuck was the last time that we were together alone. Alone? Well, the presence of that passive hole, that piece of fuckable furniture that was a substitute for Cynthia did not amount to a real person!

Any man or woman who just *allowed* themselves to become a number was not worthy of respect!

I rushed hither and thither, organised and completed the plans for the wedding and spent my idle moments thinking of how I would soon at last be the partner of a perfect lover. We discussed the details of the ceremony and all that would go with it and a week later I found myself sitting in that limousine again, waiting to be transported to the place where we were to be married.

*****

I was with my best man, both of us decked in morning suits and ready for the trip to the church. We checked the rings, he congratulated me on my bride and I felt a tide of need and anxiety fill me with nervousness. The car slid into the traffic and I was on my way, staring out of the window at all of the people who strolled through the centre of New York, filled the sidewalks and lived their hum-drum lives.

I glanced at the chauffeur that Irene had supplied, a woman who handled the car with ease and made the trip a smooth jaunt in a bubble of noiseless tranquility. Finally the limo slid up to the front of the small gothic church steps at precisely the appropriate time and it had begun.

I stepped from the car with my best man and shook the hands of my friends and relations that were already there to greet the happy groom. Behind that group of friendly faces stood Cynthia's invited guests. A formidable female cadre, all women, most of whom I did not recognise. Irene, Veronica and a couple of others who deigned to allow me to kiss their cheeks and greet them as well as all the others with whom I shook hands as they were introduced.

It was like a dream, a waking trance as I stepped into the quiet of the church and headed to the top of the aisle to stand waiting for the arrival of the bride and her maid of honour.

She was fashionably late. Eight minutes to indicate her sway, eight minutes while my erection came and went unnoticed by all, but me. The thought of having her, the obsession that she had worked on my mind, the craving that she awoke in me. The thought passed through my head and then the door opened and she was there.

Dressed in red and black. Lace, silk and taffeta, a small lace bag in her gloved hands, a radiant smile on her lips and a single silent companion standing behind in white sheer silk. A woman that I had never met before, a middle-aged woman, attractive and towered over the tiny bride. The maid of honour, a vixen who had a stern look on her face and tight lips that signified disdain as she looked around the small church and surveyed the guests. They were all soaking in the magnetism of the bride who looked resplendent as she rearranged her dress and then slowly floated down the aisle.

I felt my heart in my throat and only awoke from my trance when my best man nudged me with his elbow to remind me to look forwards at the altar and not at the bride who was being brought to me.

The priest smiled and gave me a slight wink and I waited until I could smell the effusion of her perfume fill my senses as she came to stand next to me. The vows came and went. *I* promised to love honour and obey and suddenly the reversal did not seem so improper when I had her by my side. The rings were exchanged and placed and we were declared married.

I signed the registrar's book, under her own florid signature and then in a daze, we stepped into the limo and were taken to the Langham Hotel for the reception. The heady winding stairs to the restaurant, the throwing of a single rose as the bouquet, the speeches and all that goes with it.

The only thing that I could see in focus, the only person who filled my vision was my new wife, Cynthia. Graceful and haughty, sophisticated, polished and poised, she greeted my family and friends and introduced me to her maid of honour.

“This is Maxine,” she said as I kissed the tall woman’s cheek. “She has just flown over from the West Coast to be here tonight. She owns the resort in Ocean Cove where we shall be having our honeymoon.”

I muttered some platitudes and wondered a little how this rather severe woman and my perfect bride had become so close as to make Maxine the bride of honour at Cynthia’s wedding.

“What do you do?” I asked.

“I presently work in a small specialist clinic on the West Coast,” she replied.

“You are a doctor?”

“Well, I no longer do more than assess patients,” she said. “I administrate the clinic and oversee all the patients and staff to ensure perfect medical outcomes.”

It seemed to me that she looked like a rather unsympathetic woman to be in charge of a clinic, but I have to say that at the time I thought her not entirely unattractive.

The rest of the reception passed, I danced with Cynthia and relished putting my arm around her narrow waist and floating her around the dance floor. As we danced she looked up and said, "Did you manage to do everything? All the preparation for our new life?"

"Nearly all, I just have a few bits and pieces to complete and then it is all as you wanted."

"That's a good boy," she said as the dance finished and I reluctantly allowed her free of my arm. "There is just one other small thing that needs to be done…"

"Come with me," she said, "there is something else that we have to do. Call it the unscripted wedding ceremony if you like, but you knew that it was coming."

She pulled me by the arm through the guests and through a small door into a room tucked behind the restaurant. I glanced behind me, all the guests stood in small groups, glasses in hand. Familiar faces mixing with those who would soon be returning to their warped lives where they played out their fantasies for real on their trapped victims.

For a moment I slipped back to the time before I met Cynthia and saw that I was becoming a part of that subterranean life, surrendering and slipping into their dark world. I shook my head and followed the small figure of the woman for whom I loved and lusted more than anything in my life.

Standing, awaiting bride and groom were just three others. Maxine, the bride of honour, Irene the woman who seemed to be, in some way, the centre of Cynthia's life and the silent figure of Veronica.

They smiled, or at least their lips upturned and they acknowledged my presence.

"These are all my special friends," said Cynthia. "They have insisted that you submit to a small test and a final vow before you can enter my world. All three mean so very much to me and I cannot refuse their request."

It was Irene that stepped forward and put a finger under my chin to lift my face to look into her eyes.

"Cynthia deserves the best," she started. "So, has she found it?"

The question hung on the air like a cloud as she looked into my eyes and parted her lips slightly.

"Undress!"

It was Maxine who had spoken; the tone was one of command, in a manner that I could not refuse, but I questioned it.

"What? Now?"

The finger under my chin became a claw and my chin rested on a single sharp manicured nail.

"Now," she said. "If you are to be part of Cynthia's life then we have to be sure…"

There was something frightening about these women and the way that they expected to be obeyed in every word and command and as I looked into the pale eyes of the older woman who held me fast on the end of her finger like a fish thrashing on a hook. I either had to walk out of my own wedding or else obey and submit.

I undressed.

Veronica moved to lock the door while the other three present watched me succumb to their authority. As I stripped and laid my clothes on a chair I felt a stirring. By the time that I was naked and standing for inspection like a naughty little boy, an erection stood from me like a pointer and I blushed with shame.

“He’s well endowed,” commented Maxine as she looked down at my cock.

“All the more reason to make sure that he is all mine from now on,” said Cynthia. “We can’t have him fucking whoever he likes from now on. It is my right to restrain that cock and make sure that the holes that it uses are only personally sanctioned by me.”

“Quite right,” muttered Irene. “He’s yours now, so he needs to be under your control like a good boy!”

Cynthia reached into that lace bag that she carried and drew a small black bag around the size of a fist and gently undid the drawstrings.
“This is a small gift to mark the wedding, something to keep you trustworthy when I am not there to watch over you,” said Cynthia.

She opened the bag and pulled a strange metal item from it. For a moment she weighed it in her hand as if deciding if it was suitable before she passed it to Maxine.

Maxine looked at my erection and laughed.

“I think that we have a small problem,” she said as she looked down at me.

"I think that this is the bride's duty," laughed Irene. "There has to be a first time!"

"And a last," muttered Cynthia with a small grimace. "Stand on this chair."

She pointed at a dining chair and I stepped up to it and climbed on.

A hand, Cynthia's hand, moved and time slowed. Now it was clear what she intended and I could not help myself. My erection stiffened and I felt her fingers flutter over the tip of my cock. It was as if the others were not there, watching and smiling as wife used a few deft strokes of her hand to bring me to a climax.

One of the women behind me, either Maxine or Irene ran a finger down the small of my back. The nail cut me and then entered the cleft of my ass to rest pushing at the clenched ass hole that was about to be violated. The nail hurt and then eased into me, followed by a finger that spitted me as my wife allowed me to fuck her tightly clenched fist.

That was all it took.

A touch here, a stroke there and then a grip pulling me back to rear in her direction. Three strokes, each firm and full while the other hand supported and played with my balls. The finger moved inside me, touching something that made me finally come for them.

I gasped and spurted onto the floor as Cynthia stepped aside and directed me downward. Not a drop of come touched her hand; everything was spilled onto the marble floor as she showed me just how much control she had over me.

The finger twisted and withdrew from me slowly.

"That's better," said Maxine, "now let's see if my gift fits properly."

A moment of cold, the chill of metal and a click. It was done! A thick ring that clamped around my balls, a tube that took and swallowed the length of my cock and snapped into place to enclose me.

"Perfect," commented Irene. "Now this little husband won't stray from your arms!"

I looked down and saw the metal that enclosed me. The tip of my cock bulged from the end of the hinged tube and my balls were stretched down to become a single shiny bulge under a thick heavy collar that pulled them down and secured the tube.

A small green light flickered on as I watched. It burned with a baleful glow that indicated that there was more to this device than just penning me at my wife's pleasure.

"Get down," said Cynthia pointing at the floor. "You'll have plenty of time to look at your captive little prick later. Now there is something else that you have to do to prove that you are going to be a perfect husband."

He finger pointed down and I watched her pull the hem of her red wedding dress up an inch or two to reveal her high heels.

I knew and dropped to my knees.

"Repeat the vow," said Cynthia, "and remember that I expect you to fulfil it in word, deed and service."

I spoke my vow for a second time.

This time the meaning was clearer, this second time it had all the meaning that Cynthia craved.

“I, Ray Lever, take thee, Cynthia, to my wedded Wife, to have and to hold from this day forward, for better for worse, for richer, for poorer, in sickness and in health, to love, cherish, and to obey, till death us do part.”

“You may kiss the bride,” said Irene.

I bent forward and the dress lifted to reveal the red stiletto heels that Cynthia wore and I kissed them once.

As I sat up I felt a hand on my head, Maxine’s strong hand gripping my hair and bending my faced to look up at my bride’s smiling face.

“I did not tell you to stop,” said Cynthia.

My head was forced down and I kissed the cool leather again as the dress hem lifted and then dropped on my neck to leave me in the warmth and gloom of the tent that flounced around her had boots. As I kissed her feet I heard them discuss me as if I was not present.

“What is your plan for him?” asked Irene of Cynthia.

“Well, we are going to Ocean Cove for a while as a honeymoon. Maxine has made all the arrangements,” replied Cynthia.

“When will you be back at the Institute?” asked Veronica. “We have a little business to discuss and I have to make a trip for Irene in just two weeks. We have a whole bunch of Asian clients who are waiting for a large consignment.”

"Don't worry, I'll be back for that."

"Perfect," answered Veronica.

"I'm so glad that you have managed to find a nice little hubby," said Irene. "It seems as though you have him well in hand. Will you be needing Denise before you head out on the honeymoon?"

"No, I think not," said Cynthia. "I intend to consolidate a little in the next few days and then we fly out west, so there is no need. Thanks a lot for lending her to me, she was really quite perfect…"

"She *is* perfect, now!" said Irene. "Smooth, white and inviting, if you need her again, just tell me!"

"I shall."

I felt the toe of a stiletto touch my exposed and stretched balls from between my thighs.

"That's enough kissing," said Maxine. "We have to get the groom back to the party."

"In a moment," said Irene as I stood.

Irene pulled her telephone from her bag and smiled.

"Just to let you know that Cynthia has kindly given all of us the PIN code for your restraint."

She flicked her finger on the screen and tapped gently, all the while watching for the reaction. I felt a blow to my balls that was almost as though I had been kicked between the legs.

I cried out and doubled up in the agony and shock as the physical blow was followed by a sharp shock that seemed to course through me from balls to the floor. My legs shook and I collapsed, much to the amusement of all four women.

"That's the very lightest setting, Ray," said Cynthia. "Make sure that you take me seriously when I need to *ask* you to do something for me."

I tried to stand but my thighs quivered and I staggered to hold the back of the chair. My balls ached and cramped as my legs spasmed.

"Now get dressed and remember that you are Cynthia's husband and that means that you are *owned* by her. If I hear that you have disobeyed her just once you will have me to answer to because she is a close friend whom I love very much."

Tears rolling down my cheeks, I dressed while they waited impatiently to get back to the party.

"By the way," said Cynthia. "Make sure that you address us all correctly. Miss Irene, Miss Maxine, just plain Veronica and Mistress Cynthia for me."

The door opened and I was back to normality.

The weight of the restraint pulled at me.

A new normality, a new life.

*****

There was the semblance of normality, the thin veil that covered my life and made all my friends and family think that, though Cynthia might be cold and standoffish, she was be a wife like any other. That lasted a week, just seven days as I said my goodbyes.

But, somehow, hope against hope, I thought that I could bring her from her strange and dark world into mine. All I would have to do was to separate her from those associates, from her life being paid to dominate men. Pull her from that place and draw her into the light.

Two things stood between me and that goal.

Cynthia and myself!

Cynthia was more wedded to her debauched life than to me. She loved her friends, she craved the authority, absolute power, she fed on making others bend and finally break. All that I had to offer her would seem bland and insipid. Holidays, a life of luxury, money and love. Then there is me, the man obsessed with the woman who was to be his wife. The man whose obsession ran so deep that I gave in at *every* turn and just longed for titbits cast from the table. There was no real attempt to wean her from that life because deep down it attracted me. Not cerebrally, just in my imagination.

So I fell and having begun the decent, I tumbled further and further down into the abyss.

*****

Being Cynthia's husband was an extraordinary experience.

The wedding night ended as we were waved off to stay at Irene's mansion until we were due to go on honeymoon. We left in a welter of farewells and happy goodbyes from the guests and Cynthia's world imposed itself on me from the start.

We sat in the car, her in front and me in the rear cabin alone with a sheet of glass between us. I heard the doors lock and could not find handles to open them, or for that matter even the windows. It was almost like a kidnap from my own wedding.
The bride abducting the groom!

Once we arrived I found that I was taken in hand by Harriet, Veronica's lover, who led me to a small bedroom at the rear of the house. Cynthia followed us and looked over the room to make sure that all the arrangements were as she wanted.

"You will be here for several days, dear," she said. "I have given Harriet here a remote for your restraint and permission to use it, so do not upset her. I should also warn you that leaving your special honeymoon suite will trigger the restraint at maximum, so please do as you are ordered."

With that she swept off and Harriet supervised me with the remote control in her hand. She pointed out the sensors on the outside of the door of my room as well as the window and then pressed the button to show me that she would take a dim view of me disobeying her.

She stood as I writhed on the floor and then put her high heeled boot by my face as I lay looking up at her. I knew what I had to do and I did it. The boots were dirty and she had me lick the heels for a few minutes until she was satisfied that our relationship had begun on the correct footing.

Finally I was made to strip naked and the door was closed.

There was no need for a key. Just the thought of the punishment for leaving the room was enough to stop me even trying to open either door or window. So, I explored the small room and discovered a small bathroom and a walk-in wardrobe bare of all clothes. Even the bed had no sheets, it was a bare mattress and in the bedside table was a slim book.

I asked myself if this was some sort of test and then it occurred to me that if it was a test then I would be being watched! Maybe? So I searched for the lens of a camera and even lifted the mirror on the bathroom wall to check. Nothing!

I took the book from the drawer and found that it was a list of rules. There were pages and pages of close written script that read like the rules and regulations of a prison. The slightest sign of disobedience, the smallest word out of place, all were to be punished, but the book did not list the punishments, it simply had a comment that all penalties were at the discretion of the supervisor.

Hours after I had been placed in the room, Harriet returned.

She opened the door and pointed the remote control at me before pressing the button. I winced, expecting the worst, but she smiled a superior smile and said, “Come along now, Miss Cynthia wishes to speak to you.”

She turned and waved me through the door with a small motion of her hand. Above the door a small green light glowed. Indicator of the system freeing the doorway for my passage. The heavy weight hanging and stretching my balls bumped my thighs as I walked, but I dared not comment or argue. I was led by Harriet down a set of stairs in the rear, obviously servant’s quarters from their plain decoration.

Then I was led to the tasteful room where I had first seen Irene watch me being serviced by a maid. I was naked and the two women who were already seated were dressed. I gave me a feeling of shame, of embarrassment laced with excitement. Somehow it was a thrill that I was so vulnerable, so defenceless while my wife and Irene sipped at their porcelain tea cups and watched me being delivered to their presence.

“Ah, your husband is here,” said Irene with a slight movement of the wrist that seemed to almost be a toast with the cup in her hand.

“Good, because I have decided that you two lovebirds go tomorrow to the West Coast for the honeymoon and I wanted to tell him that all the arrangements have been made for him to enjoy a special stay with you in Ocean Bay.”

I had so much to ask, but I noticed that Irene had her phone in her hand and the screen displayed the app that could punish me with a small stroke of her finger.

“Please, Miss,” I said.

The finger stroked the screen in a casual motion that seemed unconnected with the instant flood of pain that gripped me. Once again that sudden shove that felt like a kick in the balls. This time it seemed to go on for seconds instead of being over in a moment and I fell to the floor with tears in my eyes while my hands clutched myself to protect me futilely from the ring that controlled my obedience.

“Miss Irene is the correct address,” said Cynthia. “If you can’t even be respectful to my friends how can you even *pretend* to be an obedient husband?”

“Miss Irene,” I coughed and looked up to see the two women resting easy with crossed legs looking down at me.

“Where did you find him?” asked Irene.

“He found me,” said Cynthia.

“I know that he’s rich, how much is he worth?”

“A hundred and six million,” said Cynthia. “All from a little program that he sold to a telephone company.”

Irene whistled and looked down at me.

“How’s the pre-nup?”

“Solid and just a bit of change, really,” commented Cynthia, “but then there is the trust fund administered by that little slave lawyer of yours, Gregory Howard. All that is already under control as soon as poor little Raymond here is declared non compos mentis by Maxine and then the fun in Ocean Cove can begin.”

Irene uncrossed her legs and stood. She took a step towards me and hovered her finger over the surface of her phone.

“Cynthia will be as rich as I was when I stripped everything from Denise,” she said. “I’ll bet you that Cynthia did not tell you all that ancient history! That soft and obedient little cunt signed it all away, you on the other hand are going to have yours taken from you by a little trick that Maxine suggested to your wife.”

The punishment came again and I writhed on the floor.

By the time that I came around again I found myself looking up to see Irene kissing my wife. One hand pulled Cynthia in while the other reached down and lifted the hem of her skirt.

Slowly.

Creamy thighs, demarcated by the black lines of the stockings. Straps from corset to stocking tops. Stockings to the open toed mules that adorned her delicate feet. Then her naked sex. The first time that I had seen it, a pouting blade of trimmed hair and a delicate pouting pair of lips that opened like a flower at the touch of Irene's probing finger.

The same one that had fucked me.

I watched it slide in and then looked at Cynthia's hand that hung down with the telephone in it. I watched the finger cuckold me, the dripping pussy that welcomed her lover's finger. I heard Cynthia gasp as she climaxed. I saw her legs open wider to allow Irene to fuck her with a gold laden hand and I saw her snuggle in to the older woman as if she desperately needed to be closer still.

"Punish him for watching," said Irene into Cynthia's ear as a second and third finger began to fuck my wife. "I want to hear him scream as you come when I finger-fuck you..."

The pain was terrible. I groaned and screamed as the shock from the ring fitted to my cock twisted all the nerves in my groin. Another kick and I cried for her to stop, but by now Cynthia was deep in her climax. Her legs trembled and her thumb stroked the screen of the phone with rapid movements that were translated to terrible agony.

Irene looked down and through the tears I saw her laugh as she watched me writhe. Her leg lifted and she trapped my wrist under the arch of her stiletto. First one wrist and then the other. Until at last she was standing over me with the draped doll-like figure of my wife held in her arms. I looked up her skirt to see the shadowy slit of Irene's cunt in the gloom above while her hand bored into Cynthia making her squirm and torture me in her passion.

"Come on Cynthia, make him really suffer for you," encouraged Irene.

I blacked out with the terrible agony.

I admit that I fainted. The torment of watching Cynthia being fucked by that woman, being tormented and cuckolded was too much. All that I can remember was a single clear drop of the juices from Irene falling into my open lips and tasting like heaven.

*****

I woke to a kick.

Harriet stood over me looking down with sheer disdain written all over her features. Cynthia and Irene were no longer there and I just had that sweet taste in my mouth.

"Get up now you lazy man-pig, we have to get you ready for the trip," said Harriet. "Honeymoon? Just wait until Maxine gets her claws into you."

I struggled to my feet and followed Harriet from the room.

When she had left me in my room to wait, I sat on the edge of the bed and cried. I know that I really should not admit that I wept. A self-centered self-pity that was all consuming. My eyes filled with tears and I wept for myself, because now it was clear that I had more than deluded myself.

I had believed that I could bring Cynthia into my world.

Instead, she had brought me captive into hers.

Maybe that was what I had really wanted?

*****

There is not much more to tell.

Cynthia gave me the voice recorder and simply said, “You know what I want you to say, so do not disappoint me!”

I saw the crate that I was due to be packed in for transport on my honeymoon. Packed, stoppered and prepared for Ocean Cove! Harriet tells me that Miss Maxine runs a clinic for the *reluctantly* sane there. A place where patients are tormented and driven to become the pets of those men and woman that need to dispose of a relative or friend. Men and women whose longevity is proving a tedious delay to getting the proceeds of some will or perhaps well-earned insurance pay-out.

The crate was wooden and stamped ‘Live Animals’ on the side. A foam interior was cut to fit my form. With the tubes hanging from the crate ensuring that I was to be fully catered for on the flight. I was sure that Cynthia would not be able to resist using her phone on the flight. I was right, eight hours of agony in the stifling constriction of that crate.

I love you Cynthia.

You are more than love, you are my obsession.

One might think that I hate her, despise her and detest her, but that is not how it is. I love her and I adore her because she is the woman that I always wanted. In that sense I am insane and Ocean Cove is the right place for me after all.

Cynthia is a diamond perfect in every facet. And should most of the facets to her character be malice, cruelty and other malevolent traits, then she is still a diamond. A blood diamond.

I just fear that I will lose her and that would hurt more than I can tell.

*****

Cynthia switched off the recorder and looked at it for a minute.

For the last two hours she had been listening to her husband telling his story in his own words. Of course there was nothing that she had not known; after all she had been there the whole time.

In the background the waves crashed and then whispered as they swept up the sand as she sat on the sheltered loggia and enjoyed the sun's rays slanting down and warming her naked skin.

She noted that there were a few more seconds of recording and fumbled the switch back on to listen to the last words that her husband had recorded for her. His voice broke a little as he spoke, a sob and the sound of him swallowing.

I, Ray Lever, take thee, Cynthia, to my wedded Wife, to have and to hold from this day forward, for better for worse, for richer or poorer, in sickness and in health, to love, cherish, and to obey, till death us do part.

Cynthia clicked off the recorder and looked at the man who still served her heels with his lips and tongue. She had forgotten all about him! Cynthia had been listening to his voice and forgotten that the man who spoke was at her feet.

She sighed and then suddenly kicked her feet, gouging her heel across his cheek.

There was something so pathetic about her husband's feeble whining about 'love' and 'obsession'. All in all he was just another of the pathetic men that Maxine would break and then rebuild to later dispose of to clients who paid handsomely for the crumbs from the table.

She slapped her husband's face and showed him the small recorder in her hand.

"I am Ray Lever. This is the story of my abiding love for my wife Cynthia…"

The recorder was still reciting my words as she threw it far over the cliff to disappear long before it dropped into the foaming seethe below,

That was all.

Now there was nothing left of her husband but the soon to be 'treated' fool who sat kneeling by her feet.

She had purged him of his story, the narrative that made him who he was.

All she had to do was to have herself appointed as a trustee of his trust-fund while Maxine wrung the remaining sanity from his head.

Then, Cynthia could return to her loving mother.

Irene.

The End

Miss Irene Clearmont:
Contact Address: www.MissIreneClearmont.com
Email Comments: Irene@MissIreneClearmont.Com

“Road Trip”

ONE

Happiness Is The Road

The road stretched into the distance.

It lured the eye to that distant location on the horizon where the parallel lines of the shimmering tarmac met at a point. Empty of traffic and lined with bare fields of harvested corn, the distant mountains on the horizon were just slight undulations that disturbed an otherwise level skyline.

Graham sat on the dry grass and drank from his water bottle as he squinted in both directions. This was where he had been dropped by his last lift, a local who had turned at the dusty intersection and headed south, off route thirty six. Far away to the east was New York, the place that he had begun his tour of the USA. That had been a month ago, sixty days of wandering here and there, wherever the urge or the lifts took him.

In general he had not been bothered where each lift had taken him because he was meandering without a plan, just a credit card and a day's rations in his pack.

Originally he had planned hitch with Carol his girlfriend of two years or so, but they had split up, partly over his craving for this road trip.

So here he was in the middle of Kansas, contemplating the horizon and the distant mountains in the west that were his target. The shimmering heat of the summer sun on the blacktop melted the view with ripples of liquid heat as he sipped the water.

Screwing closed the lid of the bottle he carefully replaced it in his pack and pulled out the creased map that was his only guide and plan. His finger traced the straight road to Marysville where he hoped to be by nightfall, possibly the last stop before he reached

Denver at the foot of those distant mountains that that had lured him west.

With a sigh he stood and looked down the highway to the east. A slight movement caught his eye, a smear of red that crept towards him with deceptive slowness.

Instinctively he combed his hair with his fingers and focussed on the approaching vehicle.

Each hitch was different, each one a quantity that he had to adjust to with the mentality of a chameleon. A lorry driver hungry to talk to relieve the boredom, a local farmer on his way to deliver his stock or buy provisions. Sometimes a family or single man on their way to some distant destination.

The red dot resolved to certainty, a red pickup driven at a slow pace that crawled towards him until he could see the woman driving and the man beside her. He felt a twinge of disappointment because both seats were filled, leaving no space for a casual passenger.

At a hundred yards he held out his arm and waited to see if there would be a response, but he had no real hope of a lift to Marysville from this couple. Far behind he could see another approaching car, another chance, a possible hitch.

The pickup slowed, and pulled into the verge by him.

"Where you planning on going?" said the man to him through the open window.

"Marysville," answered Graham with a smile. "If you're going that way."

"Near Washington's where we're heading."

"That's even better," said Graham.

"You'd better get in then…"

The door of the pickup opened and the man got out. Despite the worn look of the pickup the man was dressed in brand new jeans and polished boots. Graham slung his pack into the back of the truck and climbed in next to the attractive female driver.

"All right," said the man as he climbed into the cab and slammed the door closed with a clunk. "We have a farm up by Washington way."

The pickup started with a clash of gears and pulled onto the road with a steady roar of the engine.

"Washington would be great. I'm heading for Denver."

The man laughed and stretched out his legs in the foot well.

"Where you staying in Marysville?" asked the woman without looking away from the road.

"No idea, I'll find a motel."

"You can stay the night with us if you like," said the woman with a grin. "Sure beats a motel anyways."

This sudden generosity on the part of the young couple was like a breath of fresh air after the last lift that had left him in the middle of nowhere after promising to drop him in Marysville.

"My name's Graham," he said. "Graham Kleist."

"Well hi there, Graham," said the man. "I'm Bill and this is Florrie. Welcome aboard!"

Graham looked at Florrie and admired her tight jeans and tighter shirt that was stretched over large breasts and muscular arms.

The hint of a tattoo reached from under the cuffs of the shirt and she wore sunglasses and her hair was pulled into two bunches.

Strong features partly covered by the large sunglasses, striking rather than beautiful, purposeful rather than frivolous.

The expensive watch that she wore seemed at odds with her casual cowboy clothes.

"We own a small farm, mainly pigs and chickens, but there's a few acres of corn as well."

"Sounds like it keeps you busy," said Graham.

"Sure does! Always working, that's us!" said Florrie as she allowed a green sports car to pass. "Non-stop work, but we love raising pigs!"

The conversation did what it always did. It revealed the lives of the participants in casual words. By the time that they were ten miles from Washington, Graham had told them about the breakup with Carol and his dreams of a road trip that would take him to San Francisco and they had told him a little about themselves. The farm had belonged to Bill's parents, but after they died in an accident, he married Florrie and took it over.

A few miles short of the small town of Washington, Kansas, they turned to head south, off the highway down a narrow track that made the pickup rock and rattle in the ruts of the well-worn road. Finally they came to a gate and Bill jumped out of the pickup to open it.

The track led another mile until the white house and farm buildings came into view.

"That's the homestead," said Florrie as they pulled up by the porch of the massive house. "Used to be called Stallion Farm, but we call it Hogland!"

She laughed at her little joke and grimaced as the smell of the pigs arrived with a breath of wind.

"Sure spoils the effect of home cooking," she said.

A large motorbike stood under a lean to by the house, a Harley soft-tail tricked out with leather saddlebags and leather fringes hanging from every part of the polished machine.

"That's a great bike," said Graham.

"It's more than a bike," said Florrie. "It's a lifestyle and a part of the family."

"Do you ride?" asked Bill.

"No, never done the licence," said Graham. "Thought about it though!"

"Round here it's a must. You know for the society."

Graham got his rucksack and followed the pair into the house. His impression was of slight dilapidation and disorder, mix and matched furniture and old fashioned fittings.

"I have to thank you so much for this," said Graham as he followed them into the airy kitchen. "I mean putting me up like this."

"It's nothing," said Florrie as she pulled out a couple of pans and squinted into the huge ancient fridge. "It's sure good to have company."

Bill pulled up a chair and sat at the table before licking off his boots.

"Florrie's right," he said. "It's what's missing here, good company."

*****

It was already two in the morning when the bottle was finally finished. The empty bottle was pushed to the side and the glasses were raised in a toast.

"To the pigs," said Graham as he lifted the bourbon and let it slip over his pallet.

He could feel waves of alcohol and tiredness sweep over him. Bill appeared similarly the worse for wear, but Florrie seemed to shrug of the effects of the bourbon with a casual shrug.

"She's a real drinker, our Florrie," Bill had said just an hour before. "Drinks us all under the table."

"Drinking you under the table is not exactly difficult," she smiled.

Her shirt was open to the third button allowing Graham to see a generous portion of décolletage that was fringed by the lines of a tattoo. He tried not to stare, but in his drunken state he could not resist.

"No peeking, Graham," she admonished him. "That's not polite!"

Graham mumbled an apology and hung his head. The drink had left him befuddled and dazed and he longed to get to a bed and sleep to stop his head turning.

At last Florrie drained her glass and Bill stood unsteadily, his hand resting on the back of a chair.

"You city types," he said to Graham, "just don't understand farming. You have to do it for years and then you'll see what real work is!"

"I don't think that it's something I want to do," replied Graham.

"You might change your mind," answered Florrie.

"Don't think so," mumbled Graham.

"Don't be so sure!"

The bed was soft and fresh. Metal framed like an old fashioned hospital bed it creaked when he crept onto the covers. The sheets were fresh and crisp and the room smelled of lavender.

Graham pulled off his shoes and tossed his rucksack under the bed. Too drunk to undress, he laid on the sheets and felt the room spinning around in his head. The room was dark, his eyelids were heavy.

He slipped into a deep slumber, the sleep of exhaustion and bourbon.

TWO

The Society Of The Road

What woke Graham was the roar of a motor. A deep throbbing with an overlying roar that shook the windows in their panes. Actually it was the roar of several engines overlying each other. One by one they were silenced until at last there was the tick over of just one bike left, a throb that made his head ache with the sharp pain of a hangover.

Finally that noise was stilled and there was silence in the room.

He rolled over and felt a sharp pain in his wrist, a cutting pain that made him gasp with agony. He looked at his hand and saw that he had been handcuffed by one wrist to the post of the bed.

For a moment, in his confusion, he could not understand what was obvious to his eyes. He pulled at the cuffs as though they would fall off at a tug. The pain was terrible as the cold steel bit into his wrist and the cuffs tightened another notch.

Graham stared at the handcuffs and wondered at their meaning before he noticed something else that had been different when he had crawled into bed. He was sure that he had crawled onto the bed clothed, now he was naked.

In panic he looked around for his clothes and shoes, but they were not there. He looked under the bed and saw that his rucksack too, was gone. He was about to cry out for Bill, but then he realised that it must have been Bill that had done this to him. Calling for help from Bill might just be the wrong thing to do!

He tried to calm his throbbing head. He was on the verge of a headache that threatened to overwhelm him in waves of pounding hurt. He looked around the room for inspiration. The keys were not in sight so maybe there was some other tool that he could use to at least get free of the cuffs.

From outside the window he heard a woman's voice. Maybe it was Florrie? No! Some other woman who was supressing a low giggle, controlling a fit of laughter.

"Are we gonna play hide and seek?"

Then silence.

Graham's eye was drawn to the small bed side cabinet. He opened the top drawer to find a few odds and ends. A hairgrip! He took the small piece of wire and stretched it straight with trembling fingers.

For a minute he fumbled as he tried to lift the ratchet that bit the teeth of the metal loop that crushed his wrist. At last he managed to jiggle and work it in and the cuff fell open with a small clink.

Taking a sheet he wrapped himself like a Roman senator in a toga and tiptoed to the door. He peeped through the keyhole to see the kitchen where he had spent last night drinking. The empty bottles lay on the table where they had been left, but his field of vision was narrow and he could see little else.

He crept to the window and twitched the thin curtains to look outside cautiously. On the dust of the yard was the pickup and six of those huge Harleys like the one that Bill owned. His heart dropped with fear as he saw the jacket casually hung over one of the bikes.

'Hell's Angels.'
'Slaver's Chapter.'

"Shit," he muttered. "Shit and fuck!"

His fingers slid up the parted slit in the curtain and found the catch that held the sash window closed. He turned it and eased the window up so slowly. Slowly, slowly with exaggerated care until it was open. Finally he risked parting the curtains and looking to see if the way was clear.

Outside it was so quiet that he could hear the birds singing and the slight clinking of the metal ornaments on the parked bikes rattling in the breeze.

Finally, sure that the way was clear, he started to climb out of the window. Gently he extended a leg out of the window and quested for the boards of the veranda with his toes. His foot resting firmly on thc boards, Graham climbed out of the window just as a woman's voice came from the open kitchen window.

"I think that we should wake him now! Fucking wanker's had enough sleep by now..."

Graham stood on the veranda and took a fast look around him. It was obvious that he had to get away regardless of leaving wallet, clothes and rucksack behind.

He started to run for the shed, the first building that blocked the vision of the surroundings from the house. It was not just cover it would conceal him as he headed away from the house.

His bare feet hurt with the stones in the yard. Cosseted for years in shoes and trainers they hurt with the small stones of the uneven surface.

He took one last look at the house and headed around the back of the shed. He could hear the sound of the hogs and their rank smell coming from within. He climbed a fence behind the shed and ran for the nearest rise.

It was just fifty yards, a short dash but as he sank down into the dry stream bed beyond he felt winded. His head throbbed unmercifully from the alcohol, his feet were bleeding and the sheet was torn from climbing the fence, but he escaped the house for now.

Behind him he heard a sound that brought him from his reverie and made his heart beat with terror.

Voices.

Shouting in a confused medley!

They had found that their victim had escaped the nest. He stumbled forward down the stream bed hoping that it would remain a gully for a while to allow him to stay below the level of the ground.

He stubbed his toe and looked down to see that he was leaving small partial footprints with his bleeding feet. Panic took him. Horror of the nightmare that had taken him in its arms.

He stumbled down the bed of the stream, hopping from one flat stone to the other to save the soles of his feet. Behind him he could hear the distant confusion turning to order as the surprised Hell's Angels organised themselves. A shrill series of what sounded like orders in a woman's voice and then the shouting was over.

A motor started and then faded as it drove out of hearing.

All he could hear now was the panting and gasping of his own breath as he staggered on with increasing fear making all judgment impossible.

He just had to escape!

A singing in his ears added to his gasping as the stream bed opened out to reveal the distant horizon. There was the highway, that black ribbon just a mile or two away across the broken terrain of cropped corn fields and stony dry waterways.

He tried to crouch as he moved but it gave him a stitch in his side, a searing agony as his body betrayed him. A hundred yards on he came to another dried stream bed that had a few sparse trees growing by its banks. He almost fell into the cover and crouched by the bole of a tree trying to dispel the agony of the hammering that filled his head and the matching pain of the stitch.

Finally his breathing calmed and he began to take stock of his problem. Simply put, he had no resources and he had to get miles to even have a chance of finding help. All the cards were in the hands of those who had stripped him and left him handcuffed to a bed.

He crawled so slowly to the lip of the miniature canyon that he was in and peeped over the gnarled root of the tree that shaded him.

He had a split-second warning of movement.

Not enough time to react, but enough time to register the boot that caught his temple and knocked him the six feet onto the hard rocks of the dry stream bed. He lay face up and saw a figure silhouetted against the sky.

Leather jeans and knee high cowboy boots, she looked down at him with a smile on her face.

“Look what I found,” she said. “It’s our little runaway pig! Time to go back to the farm little piggy, time to get slaughtered!”

THREE

The Low Road

With his wrists in cuffs, no longer wrapped in the sheet, Graham stumbled to keep up with the young girl who had captured him. His feet hurt so badly but she had pulled a thin rope through the cuffs and almost dragged him at her speed.

He was led to the sway of her hips; the firm tread of her boots and the slight tugs that she gave on the rope. She wore a loose shirt that was open almost to her waist. As she had cuffed him, Graham had had a glimpse of round breasts that were covered by a slew of tattoos that formed a mismatched jigsaw of roses, skulls and words across that soft skin.

He could not resist, he was too shocked by his fall and the events of the last hour to put up any resistance. He was hers to pull behind her like a stray puppy that had been rounded up at the end of the garden after a short pursuit.

As the owner and the leashed pup entered the yard a group of two men and three women whooped with cat calls and wolf whistles at the bizarre pair, one naked and hand cuffed, the other a smiling woman in her twenties who took a small ironic bow and gave a jerk on the rope as she did so to make Graham stumble and fall to his knees in the dust.

"Why are you doing this?" he cried plaintively as he rested on palms and knees at the feet of the woman who held the rope. "What have I done?"

"It's not what you've done, darling," said his captor. "This is more about what you will do…"

Tears welled in his eyes as he looked up at her face for a sign of pity or perhaps kindness, but all he saw was triumph and harshness.

"Please..."

Graham felt a tap on the shoulder and he looked up to see Florrie smiling down at him. It was not a pleasant smile it was more like satisfaction that he had been caught.

"Can't have our little piglet running away can we?" she asked rhetorically. "You are worth more than you imagine."

"What do you mean?" asked Graham.

There was a pause and then she struck. A slap that was almost as hard as a punch, broadside to the face with her open hand it left his head reeling from the force of the blow.

"You belong to us now," she said. "You are ours to prepare and sell; you are just meat like all the other pigs on this farm. We run a few businesses between here and Denver. Fuck-pigs is just one of them, so be a good little piglet and shut the fucking fuck up!"

Her boot lifted from the dust and took a little kick between his open thighs. The toe caught his balls making him cry with pain as she laughed. Her foot lifted and came down to rest on his thigh with a finality that signified ownership.

"You go to Nebraska for some training with some friends of ours and then we will sell you on. Possibly to Mexico or possibly somewhere else. Maybe we will keep you, who knows where your road trip will end."

He looked up at her, the tight leather of her jeans and the half open shirt, her breasts adorned with a mass of smudged tattoos and writing. Her face was attractive there was no denying it, but the look on her face was hard and uncompromising.

"Tonight you are the entertainment for all of us," she said, "and we are pretty demanding so expect to have a busy night."

Florrie took the rope from the hand of the woman who had recaptured Graham and passed it to on to Bill, one of only two men present.

“Hang him up to wait for us,” said Florrie as she handed the lead to her boyfriend.

“With the pigs?” he asked.

“Don’t be so fucking stupid, Bill! I don’t want him covered with pig shit, put him with the others.”

Graham was led by Bill towards the pig shed. He stumbled behind as a door was opened that led down some steps into some sort of a cellar. The air was cool and for the first time Graham felt a shiver run over his naked body as he was led down twenty steps into a room that was lined with wire cages.

Most were empty and their doors swung wide with opened padlocks hanging waiting from the clasps. Graham caught a glimpse of two women in the cages. Naked and fearful, they looked at Bill and his captive and retreated to the back of their small cages as though they could hide from their owner.

“Brought you some company,” said Bill as he pulled down a hook from the ceiling. “He won’t be here long!”

Hooking the loop of rope that was Graham’s leash onto the hook he pulled the chain and Graham was pulled up by his wrists. The chain rattled through the block and tackle with a sawing sound until Graham was standing on his toes with his hands stretched above his head. The pain from the cuffs that bit his wrists was agony and Graham let out a groan as most of his weight hung from the steel manacles.

“Moan all you like, pig,” said Bill. “You’ll be screaming louder still when the girls get their hands on you!”

With that last comment he punched Graham hard in the stomach making him retch and cough as his stricken body tried to double up but stopped when all of his weight hung from his wrists.
"See you in a few hours, fuck pig!"

The door at the top of the stairs closed with a grim finality leaving Graham to be sick in the dark. Fear, the punch and the pain made him vomit the meagre contents of his stomach. The taste of bile in his mouth burned his tongue and lips as a thing liquid dribbled in stately progress from chin to groin and down his left leg to trickle at last to his foot and onto the hard stone floor.

At last it was over and the taste receded in his mouth to become a sour, bitter slobber that dripped from his lips. He managed to position himself and the rope gave a little to allow him to stand on the soles of his feet and rest the terrible biting cuffs on his wrists.

At last he understood what was happening, he had been taken by a biker-gang, a minor corps of the criminal underworld that straddled the nether regions between illegality and legitimacy. While they dealt in drugs, white-slaves, extortion and murder they posed as a club of bikers, a society of the road.

This gang was largely female it seemed, but that made no difference to Graham's situation, he was nothing more than a chance captive that they had stumbled upon on the road.

He groaned as he moved a little to further relieve the pain in his arms and found firm footing.

"Who are you?"

The question came out of the dark, from one of the women held in the cages that Graham had seen built around the walls.

"Graham. Graham Kleist."

"My name is Gerda," said the disembodied voice in a rather plaintive tone from the darkness. "I have been here for a week now. At least I think that it is a week, it is so difficult to tell when you are only taken out and used at night and there is no regularity."

Gerda started to sob and it was five minutes before she began to speak again.

"I have to talk because we have to know what the victim's names are. That way if just one of us escapes they can go to the police and help get the others rescued."

Another woman's voice piped up from the total blackness.

"I'm not sure that I even remember my name anymore," she said with a sob in her voice. "It feels like I have been trapped in this cage forever. Soon they will come again and do more horrible things to me and I will be put back in the cage ready for use, ready for more abuse."

"There were five of us here just a little while ago," said Gerda. "Three men and us two women."

The other woman sobbed and then spoke a few words; "They told me that they were going to sell me to make snuff films…"

Her words hung on the air and Graham expected her to continue but there was just a silence, expectant and pregnant with fear. On the one hand Graham did not want to know what the future held. It was sure to be grim and painful. On the other he wanted to know what was going to happen, he had to know!

"Gerda, how did you get here? I was hitchhiking and took a ride from them. They got me drunk and I wound up in a cage."

Gerda sighed.

"I suppose that it will pass the time to tell you how I got here, in a cage in godforsaken Kansas," she said.

*****

Gerda's Story

"Back in about two thousand and five I passed my exam for the bar and was finally allowed to practice as a lawyer," she started. "I took the exam rather late because I failed twice, but third was best and I passed with flying colours."

As Gerda told her tale her voice calmed, the occasional sob broke into the story, but she warmed to telling the narrative. Occasionally Graham grunted to show her that he was listening and offer encouragement.

"I passed in Boston but I finally got a job in Topeka. Of course it was a long way to head out west, but the job was good and I got on the train. For about a year I worked quietly there doing all the things that a legal secretary does. You know filing and preparation and some of the background stuff on the cases.

It was pretty clear that I was going nowhere in Johnston, Black & Capelli so I applied to the public prosecutor's office in Topeka. To my surprise I got a job in the Asset Forfeitures Division helping seize the assets of criminals and drugs gangs.

The work is pretty involved, but interesting. I hooked up with one of the lawyers who works there, Steven Houghtonstone. I even moved in with him and it all seemed rosy for a couple of years. Then came the case against the White Angels. They were running the drugs and prostitution scene in east Kansas and Illinois. There was huge bust and half the gang ended up in state prisons.

They were kidnapping women for the brothels, shipping and transporting drugs and doing money laundering for some people in New York that we never managed to pin down.

I traced money that was moving to New York and Boston from Topeka. It was incredible the amounts. Millions of Dollars moved through banks and by couriers. The Asset Forfeitures Division traced and seized the money and I turned out to be the star witness that explained how the phone taps tied into the actual money.

I worked so hard at it, by night on the computer, by day interviewing and linking the string of couriers, eighty of them all together. Steve, my boyfriend, worked with me and helped join the dots.

How could I know that he was involved with the White Angels?

Fucking cunt!

Every move that I made, every line of investigation that I followed revealed a few small time criminals and money launderers, but no big fish at all, because Steve was always ahead of the game. That fucking little shit screwed me at night and screwed up my work during the day.

One Monday morning I used his laptop and found a list of telephone numbers. I am working with numbers all the time, and I have a good memory for figures, it meant that I recognised the third on the list as one that belonged to one of the crooked sharks that the White Angels used to cover court appearances.

Like a fool I confronted Steve at midday when we met up. He looked shocked and almost frightened, especially when I told him that I was going straight to the office and our boss with his laptop. We finished the meal and I said my goodbyes, I was so mad at him that I hurried to the office in Quincy Street.

It was like one of those actions movies because I was half way there, waiting at the lights of Seventh and South Kansas when a van pulled up and I was snatched from the street in broad daylight."

There was a slight pause before Gerda continued.

"There were two of them in the van, a woman and a man, both White Angels. They cuffed me to the wooden panels in the van as it worked its way out of the city and headed north. I know that it was north because we went over the river.

They took me to an isolated farm and chained me up in a barn. I tried threatening them and tried to talk them out of it, but they never said a word in reply. I lay in the barn for a day before a car pulled up and there was Steve and a middle aged woman who I did not recognise.

She seemed to be in charge and Steve deferred to her in everything. He seemed pleased to be able to pass me off as a threat that he had eliminated, but she really burst his bubble!

'Steve, you are a total fucking incompetent,' she said in a strong New York accent as she looked at the laptop and realised how easily I had stumbled on his little secret.

'Yes, you saved the day, but only because you dropped us in the shit in the first place! You are so totally incompetent…'

Steve looked crestfallen and said: 'Irene, I apologise but…'

That's how I know her name, 'Irene'.

She was about one hundred and fifty pounds and was dressed like a million dollars and maybe fifty, fifty five. Not once had I seen an 'Irene' on any list from the White Angel case and I was even allowed to see the FBI case notes. I know that I'd remember because I have an Aunt called Irene and I always thought that the name was so old fashioned and pretty cute.

Anyway she dressed him down and threatened him like a mother scolds a small child before ordering him to kneel in the dust that covered the floor of the barn. I think that he thought that she was going to kill him. I would not have put it past her to pull a pistol from her suit pocket and blow his fucking head off.

She seemed so intense, but she just turned to me.

'What are we going to do with you now?' she asked and looked me over like a farmer checks out his cattle.

A small signal and the two silent women who had kidnapped me came and stripped me naked in several savage pulls on my clothes.

'Not bad at all,' said Irene. 'Worth a few tens of thousands to the right man, no doubt. Mmm, nice tits and long legs, she would be ideal material. There are some women who would just love to own a piece of ass like you. On the other hand you are going to cost us much more if you manage to speak to the wrong person, so you'll just have to be disposed of.'

I felt a chill go through my body and my knees gave way.

'Please,' I said. 'I promise…'

'You promise what, dear?' she asked. 'That you'll be a good girl?'

She looked down at Steve grovelling in the dust and moved her foot slightly forward.

I'll never forget it, what happened next, because Steve bent and kissed her feet, dust and all! Like a little puppy, the man who I had been thinking about marrying, kissed her foot until she withdrew the shoe and looked up to smile at me.

It was a triumphant smile.

'Steve is a good boy, he will do as I tell him,' she said. 'Men who do as they are told get some rewards in my world. I have not decided what to do with him; but you can see that you mean nothing to him compared to his dread that I might wish to punish him. Isn't that so Steven?'

'I will do whatever you command, Irene,' he mumbled as he looked up at her.

'I know that you will, my dear, you are so useful at the moment that I may just decide to delay your punishment for all those mistakes. Fancy being so careless as to use my name in front of this bitch! Now I have to get rid of her! Be warned that if you make just one more error you will be disposed so very easily. I am so scrupulous in covering my tracks and you fuck it up like this!'

Irene turned back to me and smiled.

'If it's any consolation I am sorry that you cannot be of further use to me, I would love to spoil myself to a new pair of shoes with the money that you would make me, but as you can see I am surrounded by incompetent idiots and I sometimes just have to cut my losses.'

Steve and Irene left and I spent another day in the barn, chained to one of the posts. I have no doubt that when Irene said that I was to be disposed of she meant that they should dig a hole and bury me in the cornfields.

But, she was so right, she was surrounded by idiots and the couple that kidnapped me sold me to Florrie. Shit! I don't think that I fetched more than a couple of grand, two weeks wages I was sold for."

Gerda laughed almost hysterically at this attempt at black humour. Graham waited for her to continue. The pause after the laugh lasted so long that he was at the point of asking her to restart the story when of her own accord she did.

"Those bastards packed me into a crate and drove me here, to their little hideaway. The trip took ages and I was in agony even though they had packed me in foam to keep me from being able to make a noise. I had my hands tied right up my back and my knees against my chin. I pissed myself three times on the way and it rained and the water leaked over me. It was fucking freezing cold and then blazing hot.

Anyways, when we got here I found out what they had in mind because the girls raped me.

Their boyfriends stood and watched as Florrie, Suzi and Jerri had their fun.

The women are far, far worse than the boyfriends! The men just do as they are told and get the scraps thrown from the table. It is Florrie who runs this twisted bunch of bastards. I spent hours in her bed licking her cunt and ass raw while the other two took turns fucking me with a strap-on. She is insatiable and terrifyingly intense. Every time that I made a mistake she slapped me until I was bruised black and blue. By the end of that first night I was aching and battered.

When the girls had finished, the two boyfriends got me. It was almost a relief to be passed to those two male sadists. They fucked me and then introduced me to this cage. Every day I get taken out at night and get to serve Florrie.

She's taken a shine to me and says that she is training me to be her 'little pet slut'."

Gerda hesitated and then continued.

"This gang is somehow connected to the remains of the White Angels. They sell drugs as well I suppose, but they seem to be kidnapping sex-slaves for Mexican brothels. I know what happens over there and I will do anything not to be sold over the border! Even if it means serving that bitch Florrie for years. Anything!"

FOUR

The Road To Hell

"What happens over the border then? In Mexico?" asked Graham.

"Brothels!" answered Gerda. "Of the worst kind."

"I suppose that I am at little risk of being sent to a brothel," commented Graham. "Not much call for men!"

The answer came out of the dark as a laugh. Irony and hysteria mixed in painful hilarity.

"You are such a naïve little shit aren't you?" she asked rhetorically. "Do you think that the sort of brothels that I am talking about are some sort of New Orleans cat-house where gentlemen come to call to amuse themselves?"

Again she laughed.

"Most men and women do not survive longer than a few months! There are plenty of women who enjoy the services of some man who has to fuck and suck all night for hours at a time if he wants to escape the barbed whip. When the slaves are exhausted, when they are marked by the scars and bruises permanently, they become a last recreation for those who can afford to destroy people for the pleasure of it!"

Graham shivered as his mind's eye pictured a place where such people paid to inflict pain and death on their victims. Were there really such places?

"What about the police?" he asked.

"The police are corrupted by people like Florrie and Irene. They all need the money to put their kids through college as much as the rest of us. The money that reaches their outstretched palms is earned by people like us."

"Shit!" said Graham.

"That's one of the little kinks that they indulge in as well!"

There was silence that was only broken as the woman who said that she had forgotten her name, wept in the confines of her cage.

There was nothing else to say except to repeat their names to each other.

Now that he was no longer distracted by Gerda, Graham felt every slight move that he made as lancing agony in his muscles.

He tugged at the rope but there was no give at all left and the cuffs bit into his wrists with the tension.

He could feel a welling up of hopelessness sweep his mind. This was no casual escapade of a careless gang, this was their living, there would be few chances to escape and if he weakened he would never escape. Already a girl had recaptured him and he had been unable to resist.

******

The door opened, the door at the top of the steps into the cellar. The pale light of evening spilled into the prison cellar. To Graham's light starved eyes it was enough to see Gerda crouched in her cage just two doors down from the woman who was still weeping softly despite the arrival of Florrie.

"Did you get to know each other then?" asked Florrie.

Graham looked at her and decided that Florrie was attractive despite the fact that he hated and feared her. Large breasts, wide hips and long legs that looked even longer when he looked up the stairs to see her framed in the pale light.

“My little ass licking slave pet can have a rest tonight, because I think that we should introduce my latest acquisition to the rest of his life. Tomorrow he gets to go on a little holiday up in Nebraska so tonight is all we have!”

One of the other girls came into the cellar and loosened the hook that kept Graham’s arms up.

The shock of release after hours of being stretched was a relief that suddenly turned to sheer pain as the muscles of his arms and legs knotted in cramp of release. He fell to the floor, moaning and weeping with the distress. His legs twitched and his arms felt as though they had just been wrenched from their sockets.

“Fucking get up, you slut,” cried the girl who had released him.

She aimed a kick at his prone body, making him struggle to his hands and knees even though every move was agony. He crawled to the bottom of the steps. Gradually feeling was coming back to his legs, they felt like lead, numb and heavy.

Graham felt another kick, this time clearly aimed at his balls hanging between his thighs. The blow was a flash of pain in his thighs as it missed the intended target and impacted the muscles of his thighs.

The girl walked to the bottom stair and picked up the loop of rope that ran through the cuffs.

“Come on bitch,” she said as she started to drag him up the stairs by the rope. “You’ve got some ass lickin’ to do so get the fuck up here!”

Half stumbling and half crawling he followed her painful lead. Once again the cuffs cut into his now bleeding wrists, the pain was excruciating but at least the cramps and spasms from his long suspension were starting to fade.

Four girls waited at the top of the stairs. Florrie stepped up and slapped him across the face with the back of her hand before she spoke: “You’d better learn what the fuck you are expected to do, fucker. On your knees bitch!”

Graham fell to his knees and hung his head. This was a nightmare come true, naked, kneeling in the dust whilst these girls treated him as a slave.

‘I am a slave!’ thought Graham in sudden realisation that this was not a nightmare, it was reality. ‘Nothing but a piece of meat for their amusement.’

Florrie passed Lizzie a bottle of beer and drank from her own with relish. Her boot moved forward to catch the chain between the handcuffs to the ground with the arch of her heel.

“Want a beer?” she asked Graham, “Because you sure look thirsty.”

Graham tried not to look at her, he did not want to provoke her to do more than she already had planned for him. He felt a fear of these women fill his psyche as they laughed as his distress. At the same time he felt an erection springing up where none had been before. The humiliation was exciting him deeply while the terror he felt clouded his mind.

“What are we going to do with this little piggy?” laughed a voice behind him.

“To start with he has to become just that, a little piggy for our amusement. Then I think that we will find out which little piggy comes to market!”

There was general laughter at this crude sally and Flossie kicked him in the ribs.

“Get the piggy shackles,” said Flossie.

“Get on all fours cunt!” she ordered as one of the girls arrived with a mass of shackles joined by thin steel cable. “We have to make you comfortable first!”

The four girls quickly fitted Graham with the shackles leaving him on all fours but balancing on elbows and knees as his wrists were bound to his shoulders and his ankles to his thighs.

All the while Flossie directed the operation and mocked her victim: “Get used to it you little shit, because this is how you get shipped by the ‘Slaver’s Chapter’ when we ship you to Nebraska in a crate ready for your training as a fuck pig.

Graham lost his self-control in his panic in the extremity of his distress and released his bowels.

“Lookit that,” howled one of the girls in laughter. “He ain’t gonna need no training, he already shits himself like a pig!”

Suddenly he felt hands hold his head and a hood was slipped over his head.

Loose at first the laces were savagely pulled tight and it moulded to his features leaving mouth accessible but the rest of his head and neck gripped by supple leather.

Once again the laces were pulled until he felt choked by the result. He gasped for air in his dread.

He tried to crawl away from his tormentress’, but a swift blow to his naked ass brought him to heel.

“Stay still, we have not finished with you,” came Flossie’s voice, muffled by the thick leather. “No pig of ours runs away from the slaughter!”

A sudden hissing, a splashing and he was hosed down. Freezing cold water doused him. It entered the lacing-eyelets of his hood and drenched his skin. Graham gasped and almost collapsed, but somehow he realised that it would invite more vicious torment if her dared collapse or evade the girls.

He gasped at the cold that crawled over him like a wave of ice and he felt his powerful erection fade as they directed the hose at every inch of his body with efficient cruelty. By the time that they had finished he was quivering from the cold as well as the sheer fear of being so helpless.

He tried to gulp some of the water, he opened his mouth to catch some of the spray directed at him.

"Oh, no, no, no!" said Florrie. "Nothing to drink yet, we want you nice and thirsty!"

The jet of water moved from his face and another kick to his ribs showed him that Florrie was attentive to every move that he made.

Finally it was over and he was dripping in the cold air of the dusk that was settling over the hills.

Graham heard a giggling, a surreptitious mirth that boded ill.

In his blind and constricted state he waited for the next humiliation, the next cruelty that these girls were going to inflict on their new pet.

In his ear he heard a whisper, Florrie: "Ever been fucked? Are you a virgin?"

Graham nodded and then shook his head as the realisation of the meaning of her words struck him. Instinctively he tried, irrationally, to run from his tormenters.

"Run piggy run!" cried one of the other girls and then "Sooey, sooey, piggy, piggy!"

His face ran into a wall and he was showered with blows and kicks before he felt the feeling that he had dreaded. The pressure that

forced its way between the cheeks of his ass. The firm grip on his neck that stopped him moving. A hand on his prick that slowly milked him with a firm grasp. The pressure increased and something pressed against the clenched flower of his ass hole.
The hand on his prick gave him back his hard on.

The pressure forced the object into his ass.

Slowly, and with irresistible force, Florrie penetrated him, fucked him, screwed his ass as the skilled hand that controlled his prick stopped and slapped his balls.

"Make sure that he doesn't come," laughed Florrie as she finally rammed the dildo home. "Now that's better!"

"The hand on his prick resumed its motion and then he felt something clasp the very root of his rampant cock. A click, a grim final snap of steel and the ring was fitted.

"Now that he has a nice little tail and his little dickie shows proper respect, we can start the party," laughed Florrie.

Graham could hear the sounds of the girls clinking crates of bear. He heard dragging and then felt the radiated heat of a grill. He smelt the grilling meat and the general bustle of the girls preparing their grill. He began to drool at the smell of that meat, the thought of the beer the sizzle of the sausages.

While all this preparation was going on Graham moved towards the comforting heat of the barbecue where the cold of the water dried on his skin.

"Does piggy want something to eat?" asked Florrie. "Maybe a cool beer or a sizzling sausage?"

He nodded and opened his mouth in hope.

A man's voice started to laugh as strong hands gripped his head. Something touched his lips and he opened wide in hope of food.

Suddenly something was forced into his mouth. Not soft but slightly yielding, the object filled his mouth, forcing his jaw wide.

A gag!

Florrie commented as she pushed the rubber tube between his teeth, “That’s better, piggy, we don’t want you biting the sausage!”

Bill’s voice came from nearby: “I’m not sure if it’s sizzling yet though!”

There was general merriment and someone slapped the cheeks of his ass. Graham stumbled forward and felt something enter his mouth.

Bill sighed in anticipation and pushed his firm prick into the hole that needed to be filled in the mask that covered the face of their new fuck toy.

Graham felt his mouth being filled, the prick choked him as it hit the back of his throat. He tried to bite but the ring-gag gave no ground. The grip on his head moved him up and down the prick in a gross simulation of fucking. He could feel the soft tip of the prick course his tongue to the back of his throat.

He could feel the rim of that tip and the veins that stood proud as it swelled to fill his mouth and begin to course back and forth in a terrible simulation of consensual sex.

“Sausage seems to suit him!” laughed Florrie as she enjoyed Bill’s rape of her new toy.

Bill grunted in reply and fucked the slave with violent pushes of his hips. The pace quickened and Graham wept as he was forced to perform for Bills’s pleasure. The cock blocked his air as it slid into his throat deeper each time, allowing only the occasional gasp of precious air.

A blow struck Graham on the side of his head and Bill urged him to suck and use his tongue properly.

“Come on bitch,” he shouted, “I can’t feel you trying!”

At last there was an end to the degradation as Bill climaxed with a cry of triumph. Slimy come greased the orifice of the fuck pig as the girls cried encouragement and slapped Graham’s ass with a shower of blows.

The cock pulled out slowly as Bill savoured even the ticklish sensitivity as he withdrew his prick.

A taste like salty soap filled Graham’s senses as a plug was pressed home and all that emission was trapped in his mouth. He swallowed, he could not help himself.

“So now that he’s fed, we can eat a little as well!” came Florrie’s voice.

Graham found himself alone in a solitary black nightmare of humiliation as his tormenters started their barbecue. The taste of that come, the glowing of his ass, the penetrating object that strained his ass to the limit.

He could still almost feel the flesh that had used his mouth, the smooth firm cock that had filled him to choking.

It was clear that Bill did as he was told by Florrie as she directed him to pour the beer and turn the steaks and burgers on the grill. Graham just listened for signs that they were paying attention to him. He wondered if they were distracted enough to ignore him, but every now and again a hand pulled at his prick, slapped his raw ass or made sure that the dildo in his ass was firmly planted.

There was no escape.

The meal was over and the group chatted.

“Can I have another go?” asked Bill. “This little piggy needs roast beef!”

“No, he has had enough to eat, he’s going to get a drink later when we have all had enough beer and then he is going to find out that he loves being our little fuck piggy. After that it’s the cage for him. After all you have to transport him tomorrow so you need to get some sleep!”

“Please…”

“No! Go to fucking bed and get some sleep because this is girl-time, we are going to play with him and then we’ll pack him all ready for us tomorrow.”

Once again his head was gripped and someone fiddled with the plug in the gag. Graham tried to move and avoid the attention, but it was plainly hopeless to resist when a strong hand gripped his balls to make him stay still.

“We could castrate the fucker,” suggested one female voice. “We’ve never done that before and it would be amusing to neuter our little pig.”

“If we keep him for ourselves we will cut off his balls, but let’s not ruin his dollar value just for a few minutes of fun,” replied Florrie.

Graham almost collapsed with fear at the brutality of his tormentors, but then his attention was taken by the sound of zippers being opened.

For a few moments there were giggles and a raucous comment or two, it was the calm before the next act of vile torture to be inflicted.

There was a slight hiss, the sound of air or water.

Abruptly his mouth was filled with liquid forced into him through the tube inserted into the gag. A nausea overcame him as he gagged with the realisation that they were making him drink their piss. The taste filled his senses, it pushed into his throat and then he swallowed. The human urinal had a need for air that made him swallow the salty-bitter fluid that cascaded into his mouth.

It lasted for ever, that first drink.

The girl who was using him as a toilet slut, sighed in release as she relieved herself fully into the trussed form that could not help but swallow all that beer that her body had transformed.

"That's better, now there's room for more," she breathed.

"Of course there is, he's going to drink from all of us!"

"I meant that I'm ready for another beer or three now!"

There was a pause before Florrie availed herself of the facilities. The five bottles of beer that she had drunk were almost too much for Graham. He choked and spluttered as he tried to swallow and breathe. It seemed to him that she had a pungent taste that was particularly unpleasant.

"God, that was good!" said Florrie as she zipped up her jeans and passed the funnel to the next girl. "Where's the beer? Let's get another crate."

Graham felt himself fill up, a desperate need to piss himself. He tried letting go. But the steel ring and his captured erection would not let him release himself. The purpose of the sequence of events was becoming clear. They were going to push him to his physical limit and beyond.

This was how they crushed their slaves.

Humiliation, helplessness, pain and frustrated sex. Forced to suck a cock, bound and trussed, Graham was being invaded inside and out. His mind rebelled but his body toed the line. That was all they wanted, the mental submission would come in the end and it would signify that the victim was no longer any real use.

What was the point of a slave that wanted to be enslaved? A fuck-pig resigned to his fate was no longer any use, where was the piquant fear and terror that was required?

At the point that a slave broke and became torpid and unmoved by rape and torture, he was consigned to make a last exit, a last profit as some customer paid for the ultimate experience of finally destroying the apathetic slave.

For now they would fill him with their water, wank him to near climax and cane him until he was dazed from it all. Finally he was put back in his cellar cage. The mask stayed on, the fetters were simply tightened and the ring on the base of his cock was exchanged for a tighter one.

Finally they rubbed him with massage cream that made his skin feel as though it was on fire.

Every inch, balls, prick, ass and face were slapped with the cream.

Finally he managed to release himself as the pain and terror overcame all restrictions. His bladder pushed and he discharged all of the recycled beer with a gush that soaked him with his own water.

Once again he was hosed down and then the door closed to block off the laughter and giggles that had accompanied his terror.

Nebraska awaited!

FIVE

STILL ON THE ROAD TO HELL

The pickup stopped moving with a lurch.

The crate in the back was tightly fixed and tied down, but it moved slightly causing discomfort to Graham who was buried deep in the foam that protected him.

The thick rubber that they had slipped into and then laced tight over his whole body, held him in its firm grip making all sensation fade as his numb limbs suffered from the fetters. The gag made his jaw ache, while the dildo that still resided in his ass had become a just a background soreness.

He could hear Bill and Florrie discussing something and then the sound of another voice, a man's voice.

"Fill her up," said Bill.

"Oil and water?" asked the voice.

"Yeah, check 'em both please," answered Florrie.

There was a clunk of metal as the gas dispenser connected with the truck followed by the gurgling of the petrol filling the tank.

"Got far to go?" asked the pump attendant.

"Arkansas," said Bill.

"Delivery, I suppose?"

"You could say that," said Florrie, "just meat."

"In a crate?"

"Just dogfood really! Some fucking spoiled pig!"

Graham tried to cry out but the gag made his call a whimper and the foam soaked up the sound.

"Well then, have a nice trip," said the attendant as he pulled the petrol dispenser and screwed on the cap.

There were other sounds as the hood was lifted and the oil and water checked. Finally utter stillness as Florrie and Bill went inside to pay and take a bite to eat.

The pickup drove at a steady fifty and soaked up the miles, hour by hour. The unwilling passenger became progressively more uncomfortable while the two in the front drank root beer and munched on sandwiches.

They refilled twice before finally coming to a halt in a vast yard that had two mobile homes parked around the field of dust. A few sorry trees overhung the two dilapidated caravans that had long since lost their charm and all of their wheels.

As Florrie and Bill climbed out they were greeted by a huge woman who strolled over to welcome them. She smiled at the crate on the back of the pickup and raised an eyebrow.

"How long have I got him for?" she asked of Florrie.

"Perhaps a week. Then we need him back."

"That's long enough," said the fat woman. "The usual price though, even though it's just half the time!"

"Five hundred, as usual," confirmed Florrie. "Just break him down a little and teach him to obey every instruction! We don't want 'willing', we want 'scared' this time because we have two special buyers lined up who are paying top dollar. Get Larry to sort out the usual bits and pieces and we'll pick the result up on Monday next."

"Good, Larry will cost an extra few hundred! What's it to be?"

"I have christened him 'piggy', so let's go with something like that... No more than three hundred for Larry, get him to be creative for the money!"

"Are you staying the night?"

Bill looked at Florrie and then answered: "Nah, we got some other stuff to do, so we'll love ya and leave ya."

"Better get the crate unloaded then!"

They levered the crate containing the hapless Graham off the pickup and slid it onto the ground with a bump.

"We'll be back in a week to pick piggy up," said Florrie with a laugh as she slapped the side of the crate. "Do the usual and don't cause any permanent damage that would lower the value of the merchandise, Madison."

The big woman, laughed with Florrie and said: "Nothing that can't be put right!"

As the truck pulled out of the caravan park she turned to the crate and smiled to herself. It was always a special moment when the new victim came blinking into the sunshine. Singular and special for her, of course, because it would be the start of a week of hell for her prey. Madison would have done this for nothing, just for the intense pleasure of demolishing a vulnerable man.

'But, being paid for her fun certainly greased the wheels and made it all so pleasurable!' she thought to herself as she fetched the screwdriver to unfasten the crate.

It took her ten minutes to loosen the outer casing and fold back the wooden sides of the crate. The firm foam inner packing made Madison's heart beat faster. The moment was near when the poor victim of her primitive correctional facility would be revealed. She stood a moment to draw out the anticipation and then cut the duct tape and lowered the slabs of foam to reveal Graham.

Still tied ankle to thigh and wrist to shoulder, still wearing the tight mask and an intrusive gag he was a picture of helplessness that made Madison feel a tremble that went from thighs to the tip of her tongue. He was so ideal, muscular and fit, it would be a pleasure playing with him for a week, such an indulgence in deviance.

She slapped his naked rear and saw that she had woken him from deep sleep. Somehow her little victim had fallen asleep from fear and exhaustion and was just coming around to find the new abyss that waited for him in the shape of a woman who just loved malicious sex.

He started and she noted with approval that, even though his bonds were tight, he had not suffered from a cut-off blood supply in his limbs. Of the thirty or so victims of Florrie' Hell's Angels she had had to dispose of two because they were damaged by over severe packing on the day's journey to her caravan.

"OK, slut, let's get moving," she said as she slapped his rear again. "We need to take a good look at you and figure out how much punishment you can stand."

In his confusion, Graham moved a step back and then stopped.

"Not a good start, that's already earned you a thrashing with the cane, so let's be having you!"

Graham could hear her muffled voice and shook in trepidation of this new female voice. It sounded not just severe, but authoritative and threatening. He stumbled forward blindly on his folded limbs and moved a few steps.

A sharp slap on his rear guided him to the left and Madison herded her new chattel into her rather dilapidated caravan. As she guided him she spoke to him in a threatening voice.

"I will not be giving you any rules, piggy. You will just have to learn as you go along! Everything you do that displeases me earns you ten strokes of the cane and every sign of rebellion earns you double. There is no escape, or chance of rescue here so just serve me and be a good little piggy!"

She opened the door and watched Graham struggle into her caravan up the single step. As he did so she selected a cane from the three that stood in an old vase by the door.

"The punishment starts here for moving backwards."

She undid the Velcro fastening that held the gag in place and pulled the soft silicone stopper from between his jaws. Graham gurgled as his mouth was freed from the obstruction that had pushed a prick shaped plastic form into his mouth.

She plied the cane before he could speak out and had given him the second vicious blow to his ass before he had even managed to cry out from the first.

Graham was in a nightmare world of darkness and sensation. Blinded by the hood, every perception was doubled in intensity, every contact and impression filled his bewildered mind. Each blow of the cane was a line of fire that caused him to see brush strokes of red fire in his head.

Madison painted his ass with pain, she laid the blows without regard or artistry, simply making sure the maximum effort went into each swing.

The first caning was always the hardest! Of course the slave had longer to recover, but the main object was to teach her piggy that retribution was savage, indiscriminate and almost random. Fear and terror were the object lesson of the first hour!

The purple welts, like blood vast blisters, that were smeared on his pale flesh swelled and made small ridges on his skin as he howled in agony. Finally she was finished and her new slave stood trembling and weeping softly.

“I hope that you are a polite little fuck-piggy,” she said as she wondered at his endurance. Most of them collapsed at this first thrashing and only got up when the next ten strokes arrived to persuade them that a caning was to be taken on all fours and not lying on the floor.

The choked sobbing quietened and Graham spoke to this terrible angel of pain.

“Thank you, Miss!”

“Thank you, Madison!” she answered. “My name, make sure that you use my name. You on the other hand have lost yours! You are now just ‘piggy’ or ‘fuck pig’ or perhaps ‘suck pig’. It all depends on whether you suck cunt or are blowing a cock.”

She gave him two more blows of the cane across his back and watched him almost fall down with the shock.

“Thank you, Madison,” he mumbled as he bit back a sob that threatened to choke him.

Madison grimaced and thought of her instructions.

She was not to break this one, but to just make him ready for his new owners! It was a new concept for Madison and she wondered if it would be as satisfying as making a man cringe and obey without question or limit.

She reached down and unlaced the hood. It was another one of the special moments that she so enjoyed. Most of the men that she had trained for Florrie reacted with revulsion when they saw that the woman who had been placed in charge of them was not some gorgeous dominatrix, but a twenty stone tyrant who offered no visual titillation to go with the intense sexual service that was expected of them. More than expected, it was squeezed from them by brutal force!

Graham looked up at his tormenter and she saw the look of shock. She held the cane for him to see his own blood marking its length and smiled to see him try not to weep.

“I have some special things that you are going to do, piggy.”

“Yes, Madison,” he said.

“That was not a question and required no answering back.”

The cane moved with lighting speed to leave another welt on his back before he could realise that it was a mistake to speak out of turn.

Now the tears rolled freely down his cheeks and dripped to the floor. There was no reserve of self-control to draw from; it had all been exhausted in a matter of ten minutes. Graham was unable to help himself or imagine what he had done to deserve falling into the hands of this evil ogress of a woman who did not give orders, She expected him to read her mind and learn through sheer agony what her rules were.

“Time for us to see how well you can please me,” she said. “I would not like to think that you have all the fun!”

Her hand slapped his ass and Graham jumped forward as if he had an electric shock. Her flat hand on those welts was worse than the cane itself!

“Onto the fucking bed, piggy and I’ll teach you how to clean ass and lick cunt!”

SIX

THE ROAD TO HEAVEN

Madison lay in a contented slumber. Her exhausted trainee lay between her legs in the darkness of his own nightmare. His beaten body ached from the strain of performing from a deep sense of fear and he could get no sleep himself.

He relived the last hour of service and shuddered beside himself.

Just three days ago he had been sitting on the side of his road to contentment. A man at peace with himself; travelling the Midwest of the United States of America. He had been looking forward to the simple pleasures of seeing the mountains that embrace Denver. Climbing the rocky paths to the summits of those foothills and watching the eagles soar in majestic arches that embraced the sky.

That was three days ago, before Florrie, Bill and the rest of the Hell's Angels. That was before Madison and her inexhaustible needs. The need to inflict pain. The need to create fear and the need to extract the last ichor of suffering from his body.

Worse still was the future!

What would happen after the week of 'training' here?

He dreaded to think…

He had been taken between her thighs and forced to give her orgasm after orgasm. His tongue, his lips and his face had been buried in that monumental slit that seemed to swallow him with ease. The columns of those massive thighs had closed to trap him and make him gasp for breath. Then they had opened wide to reveal a dark tunnel that needed filling.

That had been his job too, plugging that oversize tunnel of love. His cock had been fitted with a rubber shape that enlarged him to monstrous proportions and he had fucked her to the timing of the thrashing of a cane.

Always the cane on his previous wounds.

There was no question of him being allowed to come. The tight ring and the rubber sleeve on his prick saw to that. Graham was just a machine to satisfy this crude and monstrous ogress.

Finally she had tired and lay back to enjoy a delightful half hour while he had delved between her thighs and the cheeks of that colossal ass. He had lapped the trickle of fluid that seeped from her satisfied cunt, the soapy liquid that was the result of her extreme pleasure.

That had been followed by more of her water to drink as he saved her having to get up from the soiled bed and perform her ablutions. Finally she had drifted off and he had been left to contemplate just how far he had fallen.

Inside he was still the Graham that had been eager to see the eagles. The Graham that had left his girlfriend to savour the joys of being on the road. He was still the person that liked to read thriller novels and listen to heavy rock. That Graham had not gone, he had just been submerged in a dark dream of fear and loathing that had to have an end.

Madison stirred in her sleep and her legs opened wide to allow him to see the woman that he was now obliged to serve. He could see legs that were as thick as his waist and a vast mound of flesh beyond that was just the foothills of those substantial breasts that hung slackly over her torso. The cavern of her cunt yawned and hung slack. Over that black space hung the finger long clitoris that moved slightly to her heartbeat.

Unsheathed like a small prick it hung from its hood and throbbed.

Everything about Madison was large and her appetites were no exception.

Finally he managed to drift into a semi coma, a slumber that was always on the edge of awareness, a sleep that was barely an escape from the terrible world that was his waking nightmare.

*****

Madison heaved herself from the bed and gave her little piggy a slap on the rear. He had things to do and she was looking forward to making him do them.

The soles of his feet and his hands showed her that he needed release for a while from the metal fetters that constricted him.

As soon as he had recovered he would be bound again in the way that she liked best and the games could continue.

The cuts and bruises on his body showed where Graham had been beaten in a savage enjoyment of agony by Madison. One or two of the stripes showed yellow and black, the rest were still livid purple welts that invited more attention.

She slapped his behind and was satisfied to see that he was waiting for her cues. He dared not make a mistake and was coming around to the idea that she was in control of every move, function and feeling that his body was allowed to experience. She led him to her narrow toilet and sat on the bowl while he watched her drain herself.

She could see the relief in his eyes that she was not using him as a toilet. 'There is time enough for that later. Having this fuck pig slurping hard to catch every drop of pee was going to be a daily treat for her,' she thought as she shuffled forward and opened her thighs to allow him to at least lick her clean and taste those pungent drops of piss.

"Suck," she commanded.

His lips pursed and slid over that clitoris. As he did so he tickled her with his tongue.

“Fuck it, piggy,” she moaned as his lips slid back and forth over her.

Lips and tongue, no touch of teeth, just a smooth shafting of that monstrous clit until she climaxed with a shudder of rolls of fat and thighs.

“I think that you and I will get along just fine,” she said and patted his head. “When Larry comes tomorrow we will have a day of rest because you will be busy.”

Madison grabbed his hair and twisted his face up to look at hers. Then she kissed him on the lips and pushed her tongue into his mouth. Her grip on his head tightened and she pulled her lips from his.

“Let’s try that again, fuck pig. Only this time a little enthusiasm…”

She slapped his face and once again stooped to rape his mouth with hers. Her questing tongue forced his jaws wide and her fingers nipped his nose so that he had to struggle for air. The kiss seemed to last for an hour to Graham.

She stood from the toilet seat and led him into the dust of the yard.

Graham looked around and could see that the two derelict caravans were in the middle of nowhere. A dirt track that was scarcely more than the wear of truck tires led into the distance.

Madison left him there in the yard. It was a clear statement of her power over him. The message was: ‘Where the fuck are you going on elbows and knees? How can you possibly escape?’

She returned with a length of chain and a collar.

“I have a few preparations to make for tomorrow so wait here for me!”

She fitted the collar and the chain and then released his other fetters.

Graham collapsed as life swept into his lower limbs and they weighed like smarting lead from thighs to shoulders. An ache of pins and needles that made him whimper, swept through his body as Madison slapped his face with the back of her hand.

"No fucking noise, bitch. I speak you listen. I piss and you drink, I demand and you serve me. Later, I might just show you what happens when I shit!"

Graham rolled in the dust and tried not to whimper as Madison snorted her indifference to his pain and stumped off to attend to her preparations.

Slowly the pain in his limbs subsided to a background throb of discomfort and Graham pulled on his chain. It was thin and loose, but it defied any attempt to break it. Madison had padlocked it to a post and the other end to the collar that she had padlocked to his neck. He was in the open, naked and helpless, yet he could not see any way to escape. The taste of her filled his mouth; the stench of fear filled his mind.

Madison glanced at him as she went into her home caravan and emerged with a box which she put in the other dilapidated mobile home. She showed no signs of concern that her victim was clearly visible to anyone who happened to pass. It was clear that no one ever passed this godforsaken place unless they intended to visit.

He heard her moving around in the mobile homes and tested the strength of his bonds once again. The post moved a little in the ground and he pulled at it with a will. Gathering the chain in his hands he pulled and then jumped away from the post.

His weight and the pull broke the post off with a dull snap and he was left lying in the dust with a five foot post that was joined to his neck by a chain! He stood and waited to see if Madison had heard the sound, but she was gone from sight.

He picked up the post and played with the idea that he might just attack her with it. He trembled with the shock of being free and did what his heart suggested, picked up the post and ran from the small trailer park, the post in his hands and the chain pulling in the dust.

Graham was a hundred yards from the awfulness of the trailers when Madison emerged with a revolver in her hands. She looked at the snapped post and scanned the flat dustbowl to see her quarry heading towards the hills at a jog.

Just north of the small town of North Platte a vast wild area of dust, scrub and broken terrain extends northwards. It is only cut by highway eighty three and a couple of minor roads. This was the area that Graham was fleeing into. Miles of rough country and uninhabited wasteland.

Madison watched him and decided that there was no way for her to catch him so she made a telephone call to Larry.

"He's heading north, naked as the day he was born. That is if he was born collared and chained to a post."

There was a short pause while Larry answered and Madison nodded agreement.

"OK then, I'll wait here and you find him with your buddies."

She put the phone down and stomped out of her caravan with angry steps. She had been too confident and so ready to humiliate him without considering all the consequences. Now he had escaped and was on the loose!

'If Florrie ever gets wind of this I will be in real trouble,' she thought as she entered the mobile home that she reserved as a sort of oubliette for the slaves that served her. 'Larry will find the pig and bring him back!"

At the moment there was just slave seventy-three, a young woman that Madison had kidnapped in Fort Collins, Colorado when the stupid bitch had called Madison a fat bitch. Of course now the boot was on the other foot and slave seventy-three had six months of severe punishment behind her.

Decorated by Larry and his partner in crime, slave seventy-three now had the words 'fat bitch' scrawled all over every inch of her skin. Whenever Madison felt like it she enjoyed taunting her victim and working her over with slaps and kicks that left the formerly pretty girl in a state of pain and dread.

Occasionally she used slave seventy-three to serve her. All the while the girl had to say how attractive Madison was, how much she enjoyed serving her every intimate need. It was only right that she should spend the rest of her life regretting insulting her mistress and paying the price of that casual insult.

Madison opened the box and aimed a slap at the fettered bitch in a box.

"Get up now, bitch," she shouted as she grabbed at her long hair and pulled her out of the box that was her home for much of the time. "Time to please me, fuck bitch."

"Please Madison, please," said the frightened girl as she stood. "You are looking so pretty today, Madison, I just love your slim figure. Can I serve you, please? Please let me serve you, I will clean every inch of you with my tongue!"

"Listen, fuck puppet, I want you ready for me! Just shut the fuck up and do what I tell you!"

She slapped her slave with the back of her hand, a blow that made slave seventy-three reel. The last time had almost broken her nose, this blow brought tears to her eyes. She stood trembling while Madison tipped the contents of a large box on the floor. A tangled heap of chains, rubber and locks that Madison stirred with her foot.

SEVEN

FREEDOM ROAD

Graham staggered up the next hill to the skyline and hoped that he was now far enough away to pause for a moment. One thing was not in doubt, Madison was not able to follow him up to the top of this ridge, she was just not physically able to haul her bulk to this height!

He inspected the post and the metal ring that was padlocked to the chain that extended from his collar. He had to get rid of the post at least; it was just too much a burden to carry it.

Experimentally he bashed the end on a rock and was satisfied to see that he was going to be able to smash the wood and free himself of its dead weight.

It took just a few minutes before he could toss the post away and wind the chain into an easily carried loop. There was no way the he could get rid of the ironmongery that circled his throat without tools. That would have to wait.

He simply had to get to a town and ask for help!

He scanned the horizon and saw no movement at all, but the clouds drifting. From this point he could no longer see the mobile home of Madison. He looked down at his feet and realised that they were bleeding with walking on the hard rock.

Graham shrugged and ignored the discomfort. After what he had been through, the beatings and humiliation, cut feet was the last of his problems.

He picked up his chains and headed into the next shallow valley, another ripple in the terrain that showed no signs of human activity in this barren part of Nebraska. It was clear that he was going to spend a night in the open so now he had to find running water.

If nothing else he had to get rid of the last traces of Madison that seemed to linger in his mouth. Rank and oily, salty and crude on the palate!

*****

Slave seventy-three was trussed like she had never been tied before. Her body was sweating under the clear rubber suit that Madison had zipped over her. A gag kept her mouth open and ready for any intrusion that her owner decided might be interesting or piquant. Extreme high heels perched on the feet that were fastened to her thighs and the zipper on the suit were open to allow access as and when was needed.

"You remember Larry?" asked Madison rhetorically of slave seventy-three. "He has gone out to capture an escapee pig. When he returns I am going to lend you to him for a while as a thank-you and I want you ready at all times to be eager and dressed the way that he likes. Larry likes the kinky stuff so you should be perfect!"

She looked down at the slim girl who was on all fours before her and realised that her interest in slave seventy-three was fading. She normally preferred men; they were so much more vulnerable, with their little balls and pricks dangling and ready to punish. Now that she had had her revenge on this bitch she could be disposed of.

'Perhaps Florrie will take her,' she thought, 'or maybe I'll just have to dig a fucking hole!"

Better to give her away, digging a hole deep enough would be such a huge effort!

*****

'Finally, finally,' thought Graham as he looked down the slope and saw the blacktop of a highway that crossed his path.

This was what he had been searching for!

The night had been a terrible experience, but considerably better than the previous night where he had been beaten and raped by Madison.

It had been so cold!

He sat in the mid-morning sun and watched for traffic. The occasional car crawled past and there were a few trucks as well. He wondered how it was going to work and what the reaction would be when he flagged down a car, naked and chained as he was!

He worked his way down the slope for an hour and then stood by the road. The last time that he had been hitchhiking it got him into this mess. This time it would get him out of the mess!

He waited by the road and held his arm out at the first passing truck. The driver stared at him and swerved to pass him by at high speed.

Graham watched the truck speed a way and cursed the driver under his breath. It almost made him miss the next car to come, a woman in a small saloon car.

He saw a look of shock on her face as she pulled to a halt with a slight squeal of tyres. For a moment he thought that she was going to drive off as he approached, but she rolled the window down and gave him a look that said, 'What the hell are you doing in the middle of nowhere with a chain around your neck?'

"I have escaped, from a gang," he said. "I need to get to the next town or sheriff's office. Please!"

The 'please' came out almost as a whine and she hesitated before leaning back and unlocking the rear door. He stepped in and pulled the door closed.

"Where are we?"

"On the ninety two, heading for Saintsville," she replied. "What happened?"

The way that she phrased the question almost sounded as though she did not really want to hear the answer.

"I have escaped a bunch of criminals," was all he said about his nakedness, the criss-cross of bruises and the chains. "I have to get to a sheriff as soon as possible!"

She did not look back but picked up her mobile phone and called a number that was displayed on the screen by touching it.

"Get me Lawrence," she said, "now!"

There was a pause and she spoke to her passenger. "He's the local deputy, because the Sherriff's in 'Platte. He…"

She cocked her head and listened and then said, "I've just picked up a man on the ninety two and he looks in a bad way, so I'm dropping him at the back of the office."

Graham could not hear the reply, but she looked at the phone for a moment and then put it down beside her on the front passenger seat.

"He's in the office, so I'll drop you off there and you can speak to him. Nice guy, Lawrence, he'll sort you out."

"Thanks," said Graham as he noted that she had said that she would drop him at the rear of the office.

'Probably doesn't want to be seen with me in the car,' he thought as they passed the first buildings in the small town.

'Saintsville, population one thousand three hundred. Cottonwood County' was written on the sign they passed.

The car took a small lane and came to a halt next to a Sherriff's black-and-white in the small car park.

Leaning on the car was a man in a brown sheriff uniform with a huge felt hat in his hand.

Graham climbed out of the car and the man gave him a quizzical look as the woman leaned out of her car and said, "This is the guy, he's all yours…"

With that she drove off and the deputy opened the door into the small office.

"Come in, can't let the folks here see naked men running around here," commented the deputy as he waved Graham into the office.

The door closed and the deputy turned to face Graham.

"What in God's name happened to you?" he asked.

Graham heaved a sigh of relief and told the deputy a short version of his story while the deputy found a blanket and threw it over Graham's shoulders.

EIGHT

ROAD TO RECOVERY

"I have to get you to the police in North Platte," said Lawrence with a grin at the man in the back seat. "I would take off the chains, but it would be better if they see you like this and not all cleaned up. Adds credibility to the crazy story you told me."

Graham nodded and felt himself slipping to sleep. Even though Lawrence had given him a stiff cup of coffee and a bite to eat, the sheer lack of sleep last night made him drift in and out of slumber and half wakefulness.

Graham tried to answer the questions, about Florrie and Madison, but after ten minutes in the back seat of the car he slipped off to sleep as they sped through the almost arid landscape.

Graham dreamed…

It was almost the sum of his experiences since he met Gerda in Florrie's cellar cage. A vague feeling of terror, a certainty as he dreamed that he was between those huge thighs. He could feel his pursed lips gently being fucked by that huge clitoris. He could see the cunt that threatened to swallow him getting larger as he heard Madison's laughter at his helplessness.

The car rocked gently on the road and Graham woke with a start as the wheels struck potholes. For a moment he was dazed and then he recovered from the nightmare of falling into that cavern that he had serviced so intimately.

Graham sat up and looked out of the window.

The car was heading down a narrow track and bouncing on the potholes. In front of him he could see two dilapidated mobile homes that were propped up on bricks

The car came to a halt and Graham remembered what Madison had said 'When Larry comes tomorrow we will have a day of rest because you will be busy.'

Larry, Lawrence!

Lawrence, Larry!

He felt a sick feeling in his belly as Larry looked back at him and smiled. He tried the door but it was locked. He moved forward to climb into the front and attack Larry, but Larry just said "I wouldn't do that if I were you, stay quiet and enjoy the ride, piggy!"

Graham suddenly felt overwhelmed by the realisation that he had escaped and been recovered by that whale of a woman, Madison. How easily he had been recaptured! The thought of that gross woman made him leap forward to attack the smug man who was driving the car.

Larry used the stun gun with a casual movement of the arm that showed that he was no stranger to transporting dangerous people when he was alone in his car.

"Y'see what you made me do to you now," laughed Larry as he pulled up by Madison's mobile home. "Now you're in no fit state to say 'hello' to the lovely Madison!"

"Please, please," begged the man who was about to be delivered to a nightmare. "I'll pay anything, I have to escape…"

"Sonny," said Larry. "You ain't got fuck all to offer me and Madison pays regular like, when I do jobs for her."

Graham looked out of the car to see Madison with a woman on a leash. At least it looked like a woman, a pet woman, another victim.

"Mmm, like the look of that ho," mumbled Larry as he admired the gift that Madison was offering. "Tight latex and all trussed up tight for me! See there's no way that you gonna offer me something like that are you? I sure know who my friends are."

He opened the door of the car and stepped out to meet Madison.

"That's for me?" he asked as he pointed at the trussed and helpless slave seventy-three. "You sure know my little weaknesses!"

Madison laughed.

"I'm pretty fucking glad that you found this little piggy for me. I thought that I might have to explain to Florrie what happened to the first slave that I fucking lost!" she said as she pulled Graham out of the car by the chain that was still attached to his neck ring.

As Graham tried to walk she pulled the chain and then punched him in the face with brutal force.

"No more walking for you, piggy! From now on you get on fucking piggy all-fours and you stay there. There ain't gonna be a second chance for you to walk."

Larry was looked down at the woman that he had been offered as a reward for recapturing Graham and smiled.

"You and I gonna have a little chat about swallowing come," he said as he led his new pet to the mobile home. "I might just fuck that nice round ass…"

Madison kicked Graham and dragged him in the dust with no regard for how fast he could move on his hands and knees. As she got to the door of her home she reached inside and pulled out a mask.

"From now on I can't have you seeing or hearing so well, so put this on!"

That was too much for Graham. No matter how much he feared her, he was not going to willingly put on that mask. He quickly stood and tried to pull away.

Madison suddenly let go of the chain that she was using as a leash at just the moment that he pulled away. Graham stumbled and Madison was on him before he realised how she had tricked him.

A resounding buffet to the side of his head and he was reeling.

But, he was not out and he managed to recover his balance.

The second blow that she threw was a roundhouse punch that caught his jaw and threw him, dazed, to the ground. He lay prone and she stood over him and then dropped the mask on his motionless body.

"Fucking now!" she ordered. "Put it on slut!"

She sat on his chest and pinned him to the ground with her enormous bulk.

He looked up at her huge breasts that were just one of the rolls of fat that contoured her bulk. Her thighs opened and he could see the ragged hair of her pussy, the dark slit and the finger of that clitoris throbbing and waiting for the attention of his lips.

His trembling hands picked up the mask and tried to work out how it fitted. The zips described a face. One for each eye and on over the mouth.

They were already all closed and locked with miniature padlocks. A symbol of his helplessness!

On the back were laces, a complex pattern of eyelets and leather cords that would seal the mask onto his face like an evil second skin.

He pulled it on and was back in the darkness, claustrophobic and frightening. Strong hands pulled at the laces and the leather was stretched over his features to create a faceless fuck-doll of the man who was, for the second time, about to learn that Madison was a woman who got whatever she wanted.

Graham heard a door open and the steps of Larry on the hard dirt.

"Looks like you got your own fuck-doll there nicely under control," came his voice. "When do I get to do the work on him?"

"Anytime you like," came Madison's answer. "He has to be ready for Florrie in three days, so the sooner the better! I don't give a flying fuck if he's bruised or not when you do it, so tomorrow would suit me."

"Three hundred?"

"I'll get you three hundred, don't you fucking worry. Larry."

"That bitch of yours is one good fuck."

"I'm getting rid of the ho, so make the best of it!"

"What? You selling her to Florrie and all?"

"One way or another…"

"Shame really," he said as he pulled up the zipper on his pants.

Madison's look was a question.

"I like the shiny wrap and the heels," he told her. "A real fucking bitch of a pro, and so totally fucking helpless. I'm gonna ass fuck her now and then a bit of oral tomorrow when I come back to do this little shit."

He pointed at the prone Graham and laughed.

“I’ll bring all the stuff tomorrow and we’ll spend a bit of quality time together, him and me,” he said.

“Fine, I’ll see you then in the afternoon,” she replied.

*****

Graham was trussed, naked and masked between the thighs of his teacher. His brief spell of freedom had just reinforced his will to escape. He had been so close, virtually free and clear!

He had to get away, he could not surrender to this battering of his psyche and intellect. He had to get back to the outside world and get back into control of his life.

He felt those massive thighs close around his head. He could not see the pale flesh, the ridges of fat and the gaping pussy, but nevertheless he had to serve it or the cane would descend on his flesh with terrible effect.

He pushed and felt a momentary resistance as the huge dildo attached to his mouth entered that cunt. Now he was fucking her with his face. His tongue could just slip out of the breathing hole and tickle her pussy; stroke that clitoris with the touch of a lover. It was what she preferred, to be filled and tickled as she lowered herself up to the hilt. She felt every ridge on the enormous rubber form that filled her to near capacity.

So much better than any man, so much more!

Her hands on the back of his head caused him a wave of relief because that meant that she had laid down her cane. Madison was concentrating on her own pleasure for now, punishment would surely follow.

She pulled his head up and down as she used him to bring her to her well-deserved climax.

NINE

THE ROAD TO PERDITION AND THE ROAD NOT TAKEN

It was not that Larry was a queer!

Oh no!

Not bent, pansy or gay…

No way!

There was no way that he would have either admitted to such a thing or imagined that others might think him so. Larry belonged to that small or large group of men and women for whom sex is not a matter of pleasure pure.

The pleasure, the gratification of sex is displaced by the power that comes from imposing their wishes onto a victim. It is that sense of supremacy that makes them climax as they bend another to their will.

Larry, Madison, Irene and Florrie were all members of that exclusive club that anyone can join, but so few manage to make reality. Madison organised his sexual adventures and Larry paid for them by submitting to her will. He had even fucked the twenty five stone woman once when she had attempted to blackmail him.

That little escapade had caused the present arrangement where he helped her with his position as Sherriff's deputy and she supplied some special trussed fuck meat. There was no way that he would allow her to get a handle on him like that, he had no intention of ending up as her little piggy. The cage next door to slave seventy-three was not his destiny!

Right now, though, what Larry was doing was certainly in the direction of a homoerotic experience. For four hours he had been earning a little extra cash from Madison by using his skill as tattoo artist to leave Graham in no doubt as to the position that he held in life.

“Piggy, fuck pig, and cock slut,” had said Madison as she counted the phrases on her fat fingers. “I want it written from his face to the soles of his feet. I want it on his cock in capitals and on his lips in black. I have shaved his scalp so that you can treat every inch of his fucking pelt.”

“Shit, Madison! It’ll take fucking ages to do, I have all the stencils and the ink, but it is a long, long job. Jesus, Madison, it’ll take a fucking week.”

“Just do it freehand, I want him ready by tonight, because Florrie could arrive at any moment and I want the little fucker ready for her.”

“OK, OK then. But, the three hundred ain’t enough, ‘specially since I got him back to you without a problem…”

Madison had grimaced and wondered if she could get away with four hundred, but Larry had had other ideas.

“I’ll tell you what, Madison. Let me have piggy and seventy-three for the day and I’ll settle for three hundred green.”

That was how it had been sorted.

Now Larry had his prick reaming the mouth of the man he was tattooing while the latex clad slave helped herself to his balls with her lips and tongue.

Larry’s hands shook as he worked and climaxed again. Each time, the fuck pig swallowed the come like a good little slave and Larry used his right hand to build his next erection. Through the window he occasionally saw Madison glancing in as he worked.

It might have bothered another man, but Larry was indulging his most basic fantasy. 'Let the fat cow watch,' he thought, 'that way she'll know what I want next time.'

Other people were there to serve him and he could take what he liked from them. He could feel another climax building. This was the third now, slower to arrive, less intense and created with more effort on the part of the two slaves, but nevertheless the third inside three hours…

He pushed into the ring gag of the prone man and looked down at the woman who had the job of attending to ass and balls. Her eyes were looking up, into his. They were empty of all emotion, but fear!

Fear was enough!

*****

The journey back to the Florrie's Hell's Angel's was a road trip of dread and fearful trepidation. Since being forced to put the hood on and being bound after his awful session with Larry, Graham had not been beaten, that would have damaged the healing tattoos. He had not seen what had been done to his skin and he had no idea what lay ahead except that somehow he knew that if he did not escape Florrie in the first few days he would never be able to get away.

He would be forever a slave slut to these perverse women.

So, that last day with Madison was one where she tortured him without using the cane. Four dry hours tied up in the sun followed by a long drink of her wastes. Then came the service that was pepped up by her use of Larry's stun gun.

Finally, the packing and preparation in which he was once again bundled and rammed into the soft foam with every hole filled to prevent unwanted emissions. As she packed him into the crate, Madison could not help but enjoy his distress.

She played with his prick until he had achieved a strong erection and then she slowly masturbated him as she told him what might happen when he returned to Florrie's tender care. As he started to come she slowed the pace and told him stories of previous slaves who had passed through her hands.

Finally she told him of snuff movies, operations that made sex slaves so much more obedient or totally helpless. Private dungeons that slaves entered and never left. Playrooms of pain and suffering for the gratification of their rich owners.

As she whispered in his ear she watched and waited for the first tears to roll from under the mask. As they did so she forced him to climax to her tales of the future that he was going to experience as a victim.

It was one of her only moments of subtlety. Making the slave climax, in part stimulated by tales of the horrors that he would experience.

Finally, when he was in mental torment she closed the case and screwed the sides in place. It would be a few hours before Florrie was to arrive, so she decided to relax with seventy-three and enjoy a little massage and intimate luxury!

*****

For Graham, the fuck piggy in the crate, the journey back to the Florrie's Hell's Angels' headquarters was much like the journey out. The difference was that Graham had finally realised that this was real.

It was his future, or at least what was left of it.

The noise of the truck covering its miles.

The stops to fill the car with gas, the painful bindings and fetters, the soreness of his skin. It was all part of a waking nightmare that was almost unendurable.

Finally it was over and the box was tipped off the back of the pickup with a shove. He heard a slap on the side of the crate, almost a friendly recognition that it contained a pre-packed slave.

Then nothing.

There was the sound of motorcycle engines revving and then some voices, mainly female that penetrated the wood and foam of the packing crate.

Finally the crate was tipped onto its side and pushed along the ground, presumably to clear the open area in front of the house. Graham just quietly wept into his mask as he realised that he was of so little importance that he was just a commercial commodity to these people, a fairly valuable product and nothing more.

TEN

THE END OF THE ROAD

Graham heard the car arrive.

Just!

In the absolute still of the night he heard it over the small sounds of the insects and rustling of the wind. There was a crunch of gravel, slight but steady, that made a noise even though the engine had been turned off and the car had rolled the last hundred yards.

The doors of the limousine opened and two women and two men exited the car like ghosts. One woman stayed in the car and watched her followers prepare to dispose of a small problem at her behest.

It was not often that she happened to get to witness their work, usually she was too busy to be bothered with minor actions like this.

She smiled and watched them check their silenced pistols, a brief twist of silencer and a click as magazines were tested and safety catches were lowered. In the dark they faded around the house with almost no sound.

The woman in the car stretched her legs a little and rotated so that she could slide out of the car with ease. Her stiletto heels found footing in the dust and she stood and looked around the yard. All was quiet, a new moon would have hung in the sky, but small clouds covered it. From her smart jacket pocket she took slim silver case and lit a cigarette that she extracted with almost exaggerated care.

She heard a small sound from the house and smiled, this was the end of the affair at last. The last time that she allowed her people to become involved, implicated, in a total mess like this!

Motorcycle gangs, drugs and prostitution!

What were they all thinking?

'It just remains to tie up the last loose ends and then go home to New York,' she thought as she drew at the cigarette with real enjoyment.

There was something so satisfying about being in at the finish of course! First there had been the White Angels and the fact that they had connection to her organisation. All contact had been broken and cleaned up, including that stupid idiot Steven Houghtonstone from the prosecutor's office in Topeka.

The idiot that had used her name in such an indiscrete fashion.

Well, Steve was no more, or at least he had been sold to a lovely Japanese couple, Mr and Mrs Tokashirimaso. That left the problem of the slave who should have been disposed of, but instead had been sold on to this pack of cut-rate rats.

Irene heard a couple of muffled shots from the house.

Like soft claps they signalled that her people were finally taking care of business with a measure of finality.

She tossed the butt of her cigarette in the dust and twisted the sole of her shoe on it just as a couple more shots spluttered in the house.

Irene held her hand up with fingers outstretched and admired the manicure. Simple red with a crusting of gold that made it look as though her nails had been partly gilded.

'Now there is just that stupid bitch from the prosecutor's office in Topeka to deal with and then the matter is closed, finally,' she thought.

The door opened and Florrie was pushed into the yard by an unseen hand. Her hands were half up and clear of weapons; her body was naked and drenched in sweat.

"Very good," said Irene with a smile. "I wonder if you could help me find someone? Actually someone in particular."

The question was framed in an ironic tone of voice as if Irene were asking for directions from a passing stranger.

"Who the fuck are you, bitch?" answered Florrie.

"My name is none of your concern, Florence Hardcampe. You are here to answer my questions, that is enough for you to know."

Florrie took a step forward as if threatening Irene and one of the women who had been in the car with their mistress stepped out of the doorway and placed the lips of a Beretta on her neck.

"I am looking for a young woman who was sold to you a month ago. I understand that you have her here on the premises? A certain Gerda Hartley?"

"What is it worth, to tell you where she is?"

A tired, bored look came over Irene's face and she strolled to stand in front of the naked woman who was actually trying to bargain with her. Irene stretched out a hand and gently traced the shape of a breast with her nail. The hand slid down between Florrie's thighs and parted her sex.

"I do not think that you understand what risk you are taking by annoying me with your stupid attempts to haggle with me. I can do things to you that you cannot imagine. I can reduce you to a boneless jelly that howls all night to beg to eat my shit if I care to."

Irene pushed her finger up, deep into Florrie and smiled as if they were just shaking hands.

"I cannot hear you, Florence…"

"The chicken cellar, there," said Florrie as she pointed at the door in the barn.

There were now six people in the yard, Florrie, Miss Irene Clearmont and all four of her assistants. Irene indicated with her free hand to one of the women, who went to the door and opened it.

For a moment she stood at the top of the stairs before she disappeared into the gloom. There was a small pause. Florrie stood on her tip-toes as Irene pushed deep into her. A small smile played on her lips as she enjoyed the discomfort that she was causing.

The woman reappeared in the door way and signalled to Irene by drawing a finger-tip over her throat.

"You see how easy that was, how painless… Now all we have to decide is; what to do with you, Miss Florence Hardcampe. What do you think?"

"Let me go of course," said Florrie with a defiant shrug of the shoulders. "You got what you came for."

"I suppose that true," said Irene as she slowly withdrew her finger from Florrie.

The hand came up and the finger that had fucked her was held to Florrie's lips. Knowing what was required, Florrie's lips parted and she kissed the finger that had raped her.

"Excuse me, Miss," said one of the men, "but what is in that?"

He pointed to the crate where Graham was stored for a sale that would now never happen.

"Open it!"

It was a work of moments to strip the case down to the foam interior and discover Graham curled up and entombed within.

"Who is he?"

Florrie answered the question immediately. She could feel the silencer pressing into her skull so she did not dissemble overly.

"I was on the point of selling him to that 'Esclavo Servil' brothel, you know near Buenaventura."

"Isn't that the place where they have that private little film studio?"

Florrie nodded cautiously, careful not to give the wrong impression to the woman who was holding a gun to her head.

"Well, Florence, it would seem that I am all done here apart from a few singular details. I suppose that I can offer you a choice. Of course it will be a little limited in scope. Either you can come with me and we find out what the future holds for you or; on the other hand you stay here with no future."

"I'll go with you," said Florrie, guessing correctly that 'no future' meant just that!

ELEVEN

TERMINI

The road trip was at last at an end.

Graham stood and looked at the mirror at what Madison had had done to him. Larry had covered every inch with the words 'pig' , 'fuck' and 'slut'. As Larry had done it he had enjoyed his victim's struggles to learn to suck cock.

Lips that wrapped tightly around the root of that large prick and then sucked and massaged to make it spew its pleasure into a servile mouth.

Graham shrugged, all of it meant nothing, and all of the terrible privations that he had suffered were of no account! Compared with Florrie's dashed expectations his own trials and tribulations were inconsequential.

Florrie had been sucked into the system of which she had been just an inconsequential cog. She found herself spat out as a white slave in Indonesia, just a servile foreigner who was there to satisfy her buyers. She would serve the rest of her days as a depositary for the emissions of thirty men a night, who wanted to find out what it was like to fuck and rape a white woman.

Graham on the other hand, had engendered no risk for his new owners. He was picked up like a child picks up a tumbling pebble from the surf on the beach. Picked up and thrown back into the water with a casual cast.

The training and auction were almost like freedom to him. After the terrors of Madison and Florrie, the canings and the cages, the rapes and the chains were gone to be replaced by a strict regime of service that was occasionally rewarded by his mistress. Once a week he was allowed to have a quiet hour to masturbate as long as he had not disobeyed any orders or failed in his duties.

She was so considerate, so generous to him!

Occasionally his owner would actually sit in and enjoy watching him perform for her. She liked to see a slow and steady climax from him while he stared into her eyes and asked her permission.

“That’s a good boy, come for me my little slutty piggy,” she said as his prick erupted for her. “I love the tattoos, piggy, they suit you so well! Say ‘thank you’ to me for looking after you.”

“Thank you,” he replied.

The rest of the time he spent locked up, his prick in a narrow tube that allowed him no relief. Up at five in the morning to clean the villa and prepare for his owners to rise. He padded around the house in his tight uniform constantly under the supervision of the two women who ran the household. Washing, cleaning and tidying up constantly, there was no moment to think about what could or should have been.

Graham had long realised that a failure to please here would result in his being sold on. Finally, a lazy slave always ended in some brothel or film studio where his life could be measured in weeks.

So he served the master and mistress as well as the female supervisors with great care and attention.

The supervisors had their nightly uses for the man who was lower in the order of seniority than the parrot whose cage he cleaned twice a day.

The road trip that had started in New York had ended so far away!

He had hoped to find freedom on the road, but he had lost free will on the way.

He had lost everything that he had once held so dear, but he had gained purpose:

The single minded service that made his betters and owners glad that they had bought him.

He had become the perfect slave.

THE END

Made in the USA
Monee, IL
11 November 2023